Sports Illustrated KIDS

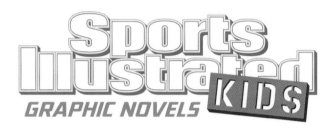

GRAPHIC NOVELS

STONE ARCH BOOKS
a capstone imprint

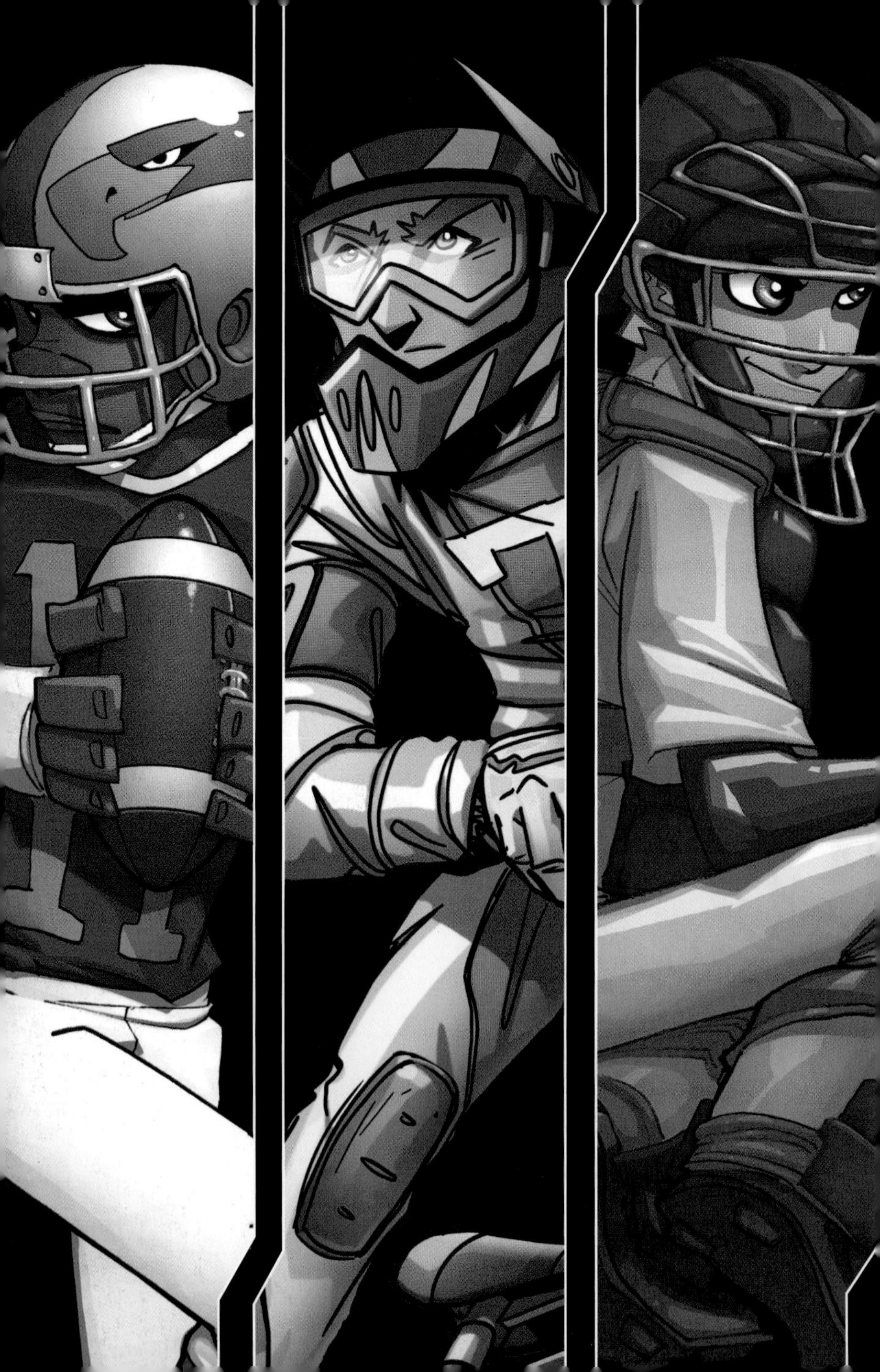

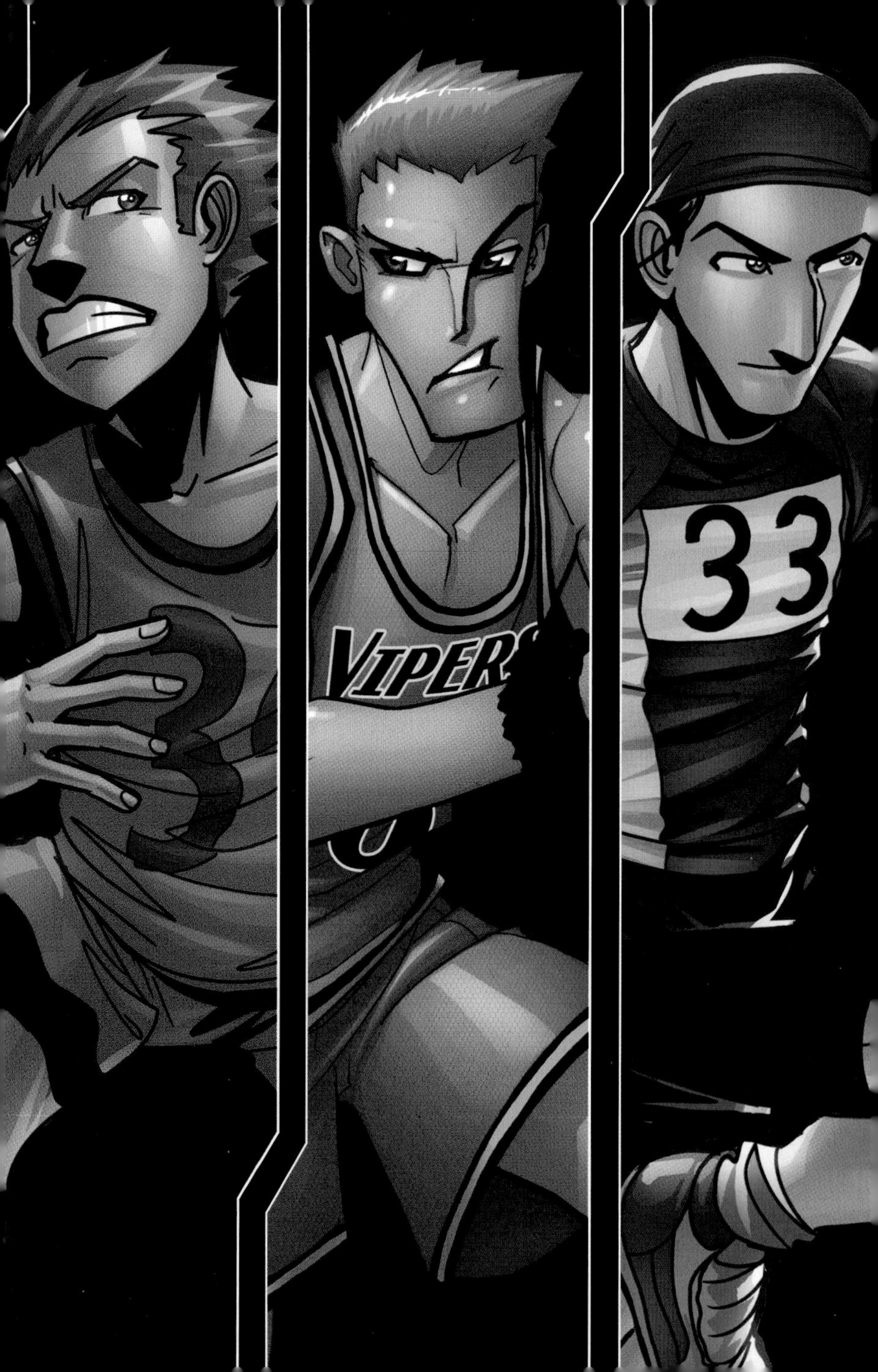
VIPERS
33

UP NEXT ›››

on Sports Illustrated KIDS

:02 SPORTS ZONE SPECIAL REPORT

:04 FEATURE PRESENTATION:

BMX BLITZ

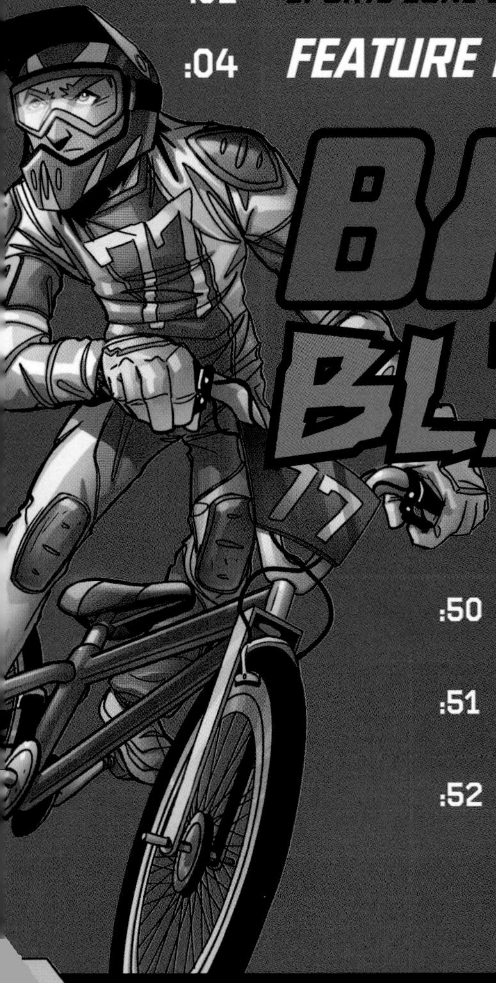

77

FOLLOWED BY:

:50 SPORTS ZONE POSTGAME RECAP

:51 SPORTS ZONE POSTGAME EXTRA

:52 SI KIDS INFO CENTER

P RACERS FROM ALL OVER ARRIVE FOR BMX-BLITZKRIEG BIK SIK TICKER

SPORTS ZONE

SPECIAL REPORT

BMX BMX RACING
PNT PAINTBALL
FBL FOOTBALL
BSL BASEBALL
BBL BASKETBALL

ULTIMATE BMX RACE COURSE AWAITS TOP TEEN BIKERS

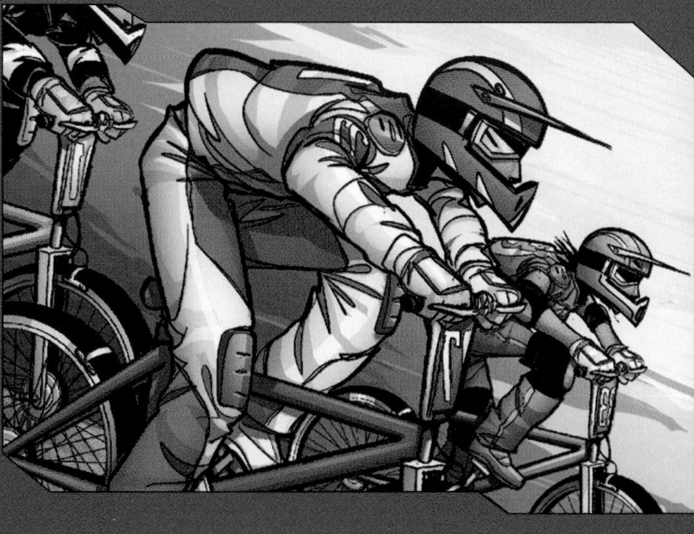

LUKE LAWLESS

STATS:
AGE: 14
COLORS: GREEN/WHITE

BIO: Luke Lawless is a top-ranked teen BMX biker who has traveled a long way to compete in the BMX-Blitzkrieg. The super-secret, brand-new race course has been kept under wraps during its development, so no one knows exactly what to expect. But one thing's for certain — this will be the wildest ride Luke Lawless has ever experienced.

Sports Illustrated KIDS

UP NEXT: BMX BLITZ

BLZ vs BMS
3-1
TGR vs RDR
33-32
EAG vs BAN
14-7
SPA vs WLD
4-3
BAN vs RDR
21-15
RZR vs LIG
4-3
BLZ vs BMS
3-1

HOUSTON MORIKAMI

AGE: 15
COLORS: PINK/WHITE

BIO: Houston is the only female competitor in the BMX-Blitzkrieg — but she doesn't care. Houston's been beating boys on the race course since she first put foot to pedal.

PETER HILDEBRAND

AGE: 14   **COLORS:** BLACK/SILVER
BIO: Peter is the son of a wealthy CEO and has all the best biking gear. On the race course, Peter is as ruthless as his businessman father.

PETER

DENNY LAWLESS

AGE: 42
BIO: Luke Lawless's father is a famous NASCAR driver who isn't all that interested in BMX racing.

DENNY

THE MORIKAMIS

FIRST NAMES: HUAN AND KAZU
BIO: The Morikamis do not approve of their daughter competing in BMX races. They would rather she focus more on scholarly pursuits.

MORIKAMIS

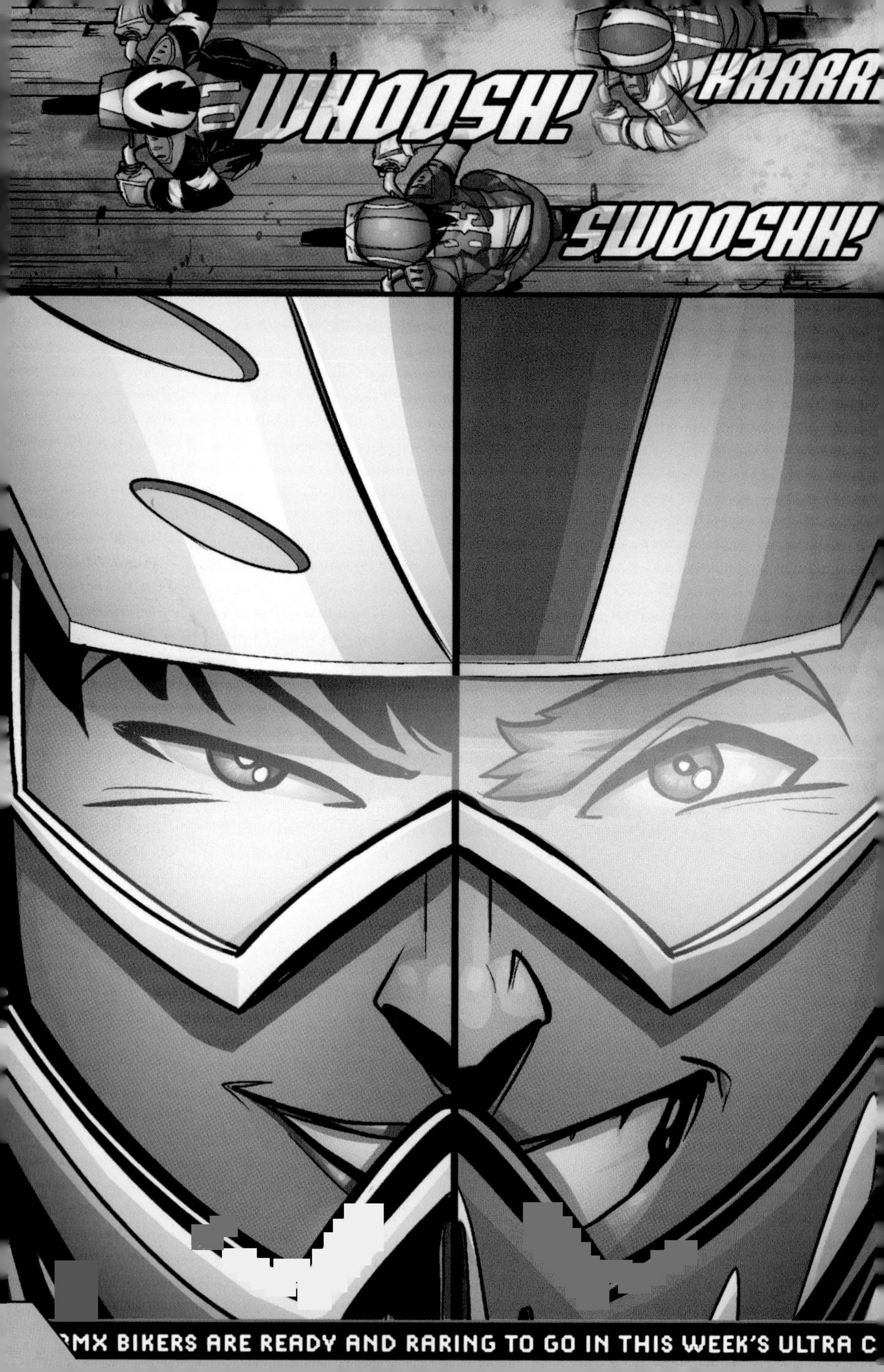
WHOOSH!
KRRRR
SWOOSHH!
BMX BIKERS ARE READY AND RARING TO GO IN THIS WEEK'S ULTRA C

Sports Illustrated KIDS

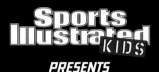

PRESENTS

BMX BLITZ

A PRODUCTION OF

STONE ARCH BOOKS
a capstone imprint

written by Scott Ciencin
illustrated by Aburtov
inked by Andres Esparza
colored by Fares Maese

Sports Illustrated KIDS *BMX Blitz* is published by Stone Arch Books, 1710 Roe Crest Drive, North Mankato, Minnesota 56003.
www.capstonepub.com

Summary: Luke is the son of a famous NASCAR driver. Houston is the only girl to win the state BMX title. So what do these talented teens have in common? They're both racing in the ultimate BMX competition, the BMX-Blitzkrieg! The super-secret course has been kept under wraps, so no one knows what to expect . . .

designed and directed by Bob Lentz
edited by Sean Tulien
creative direction by Heather Kindseth
editorial management by Donald Lemke
editorial direction by Michael Dahl

Library of Congress Cataloging-in-Publication Data
Ciencin, Scott.
BMX blitz / written by Scott Ciencin ; illustrated by Aburtov ; illustrated by Andres Esparza ; illustrated by Fares Maese.
p. cm. -- (Sports Illustrated kids graphic novels)
ISBN 978-1-4342-2222-0 (library binding)
ISBN 978-1-4342-3071-3 (paperback)
ISBN 978-1-4342-4940-1 (e-book)
1. Graphic novels. [1. Graphic novels. 2. Bicycle motocross--Fiction. 3. Competition (Psychology)--Fiction. 4. Cheating--Fiction.] I. Aburto, Jesus, ill. II. Esparza, Andres, ill. III. Maese, Fares, ill. IV. Title.
PZ7.7.C54Bm 2011
741.5'973--dc22 2010032425

Printed in the United States of America in North Mankato, Minnesota.
122017 010973R

TITIVE RACE FEATURING THE BMX-BLITZKRIEG SUPER-COURS SIK TICKER

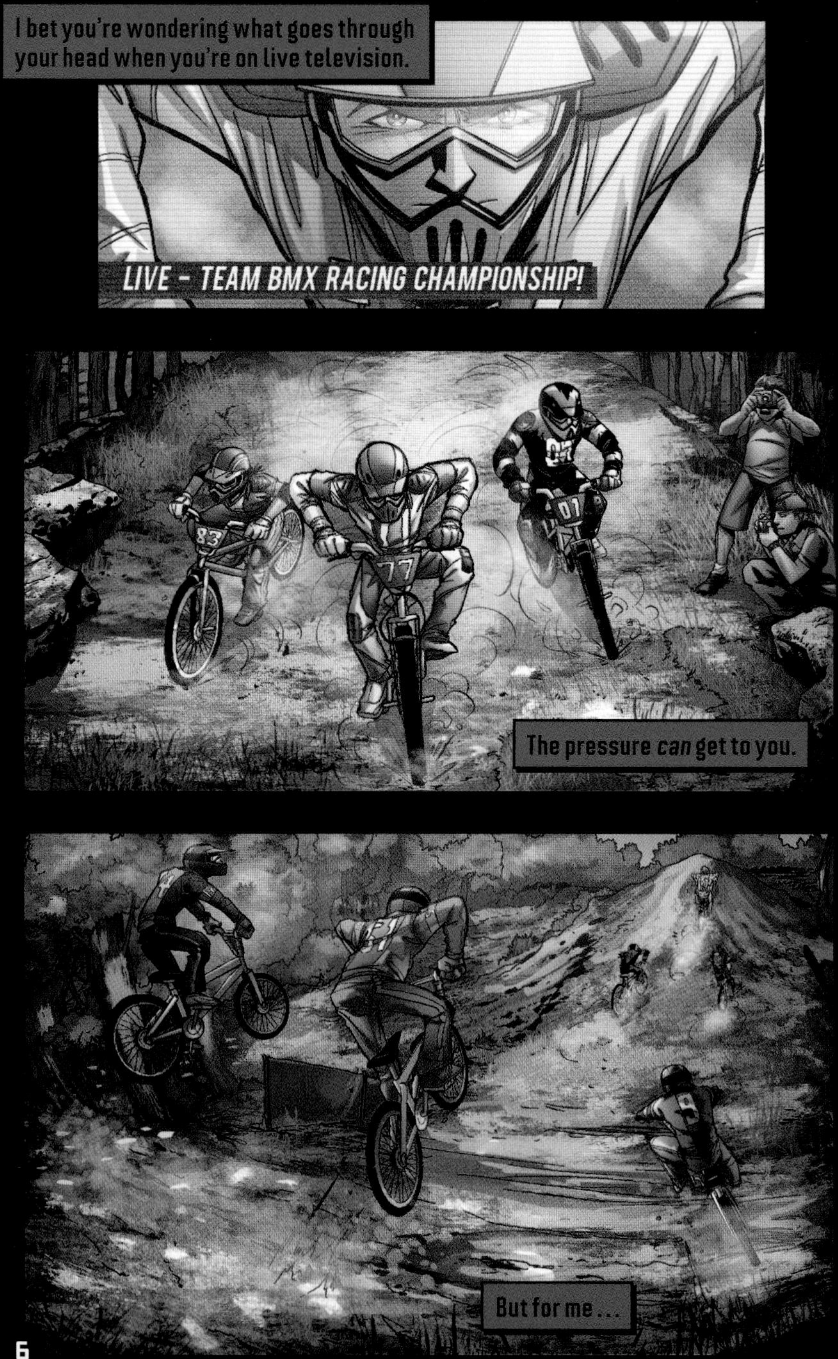
I bet you're wondering what goes through your head when you're on live television.
LIVE – TEAM BMX RACING CHAMPIONSHIP!
83
77
01
The pressure *can* get to you.
But for me . . .

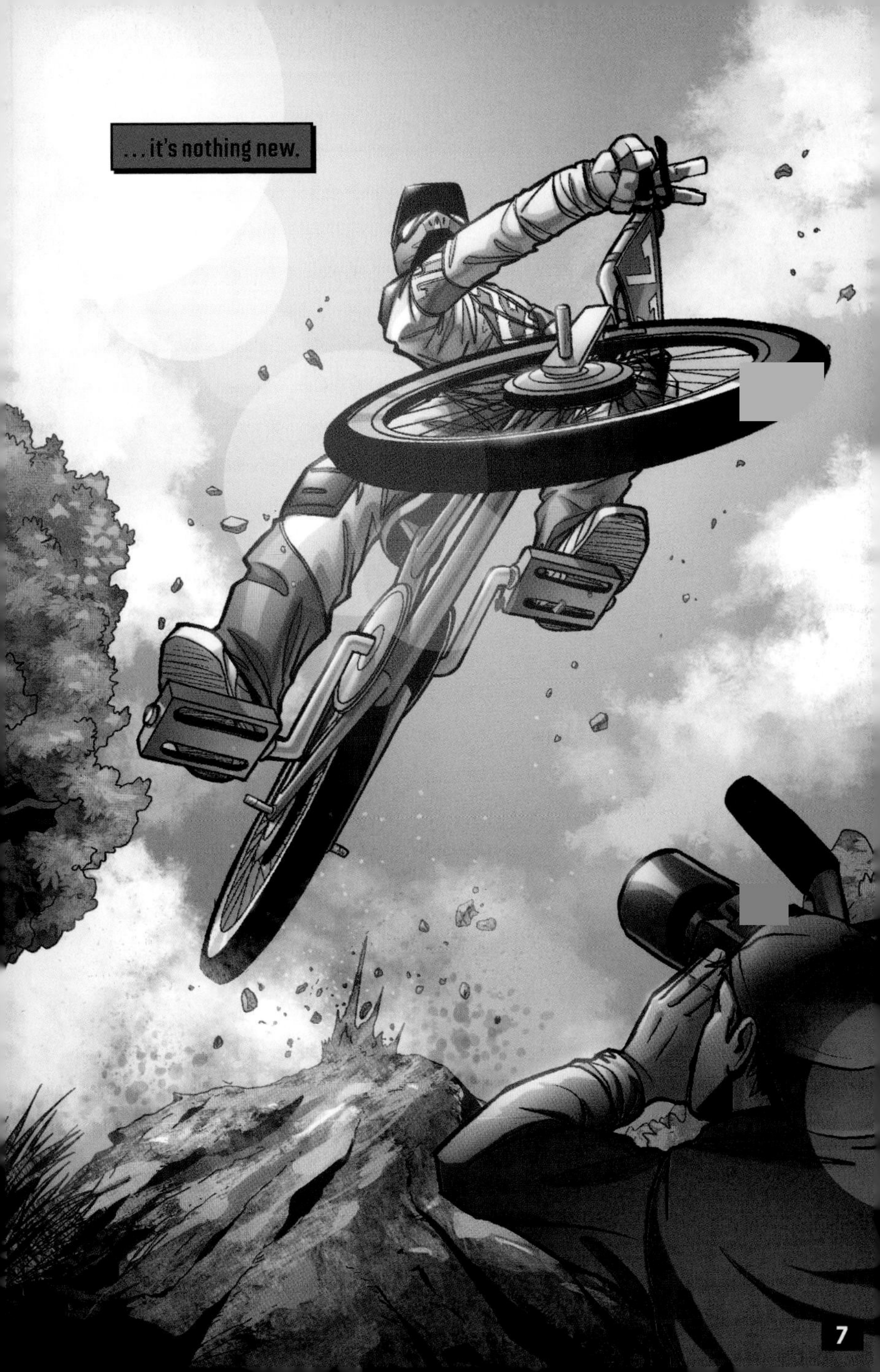
. . . it's nothing new.

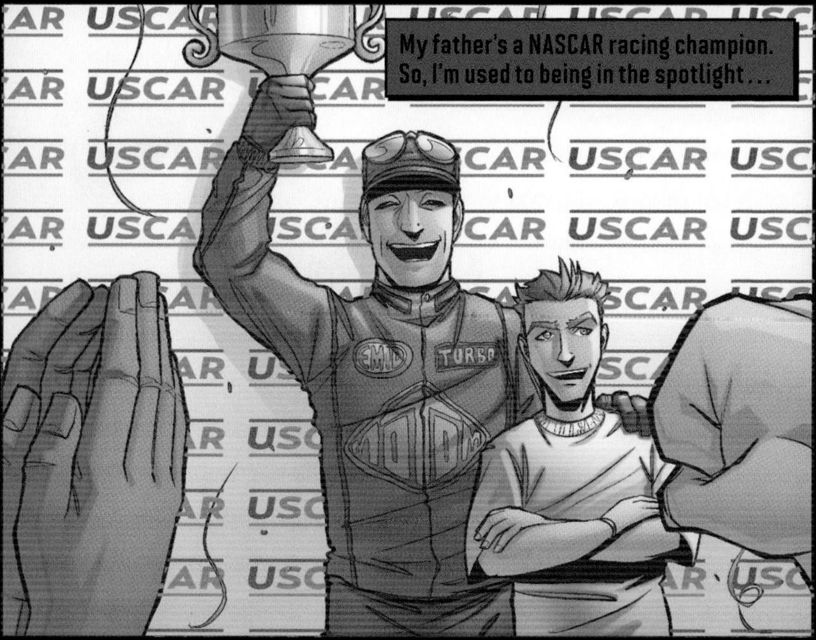
My father's a NASCAR racing champion. So, I'm used to being in the spotlight . . .
USCAR
EMID
TURBO

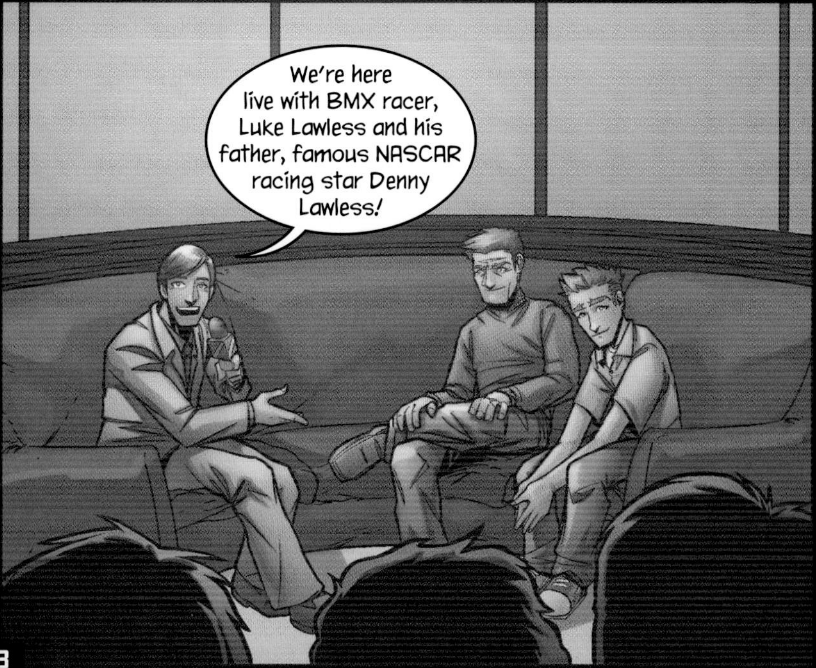
We're here live with BMX racer, Luke Lawless and his father, famous NASCAR racing star Denny Lawless!

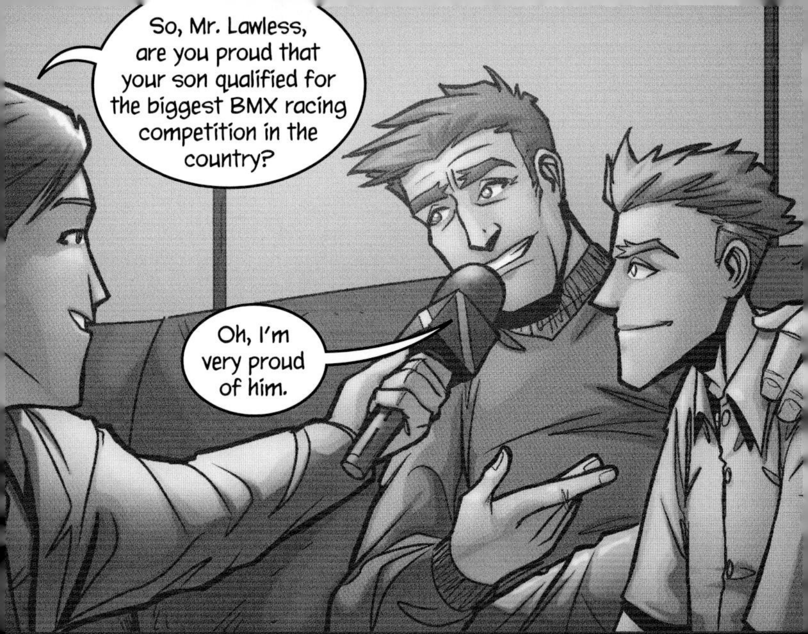
So, Mr. Lawless, are you proud that your son qualified for the biggest BMX racing competition in the country?
Oh, I'm very proud of him.
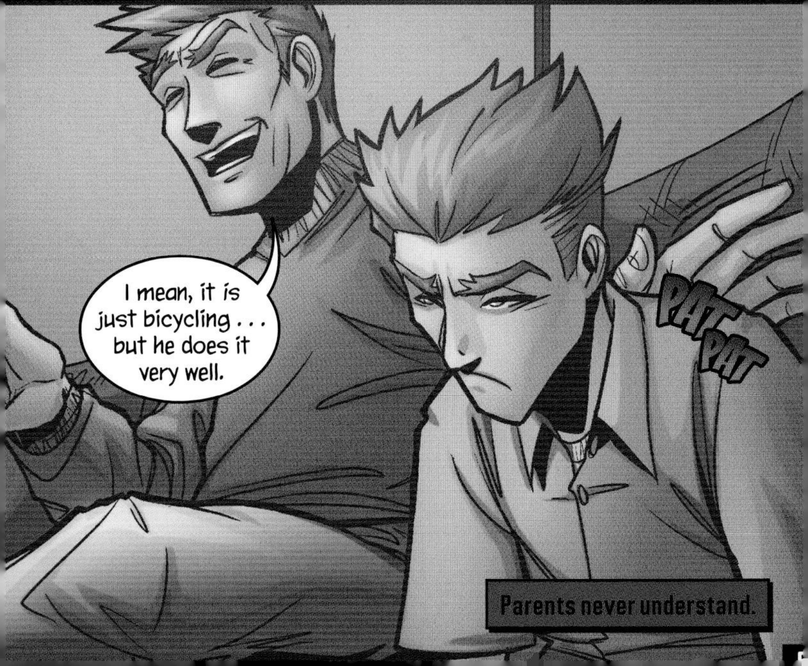
I mean, it is just bicycling . . . but he does it very well.
PAT PAT
Parents never understand.

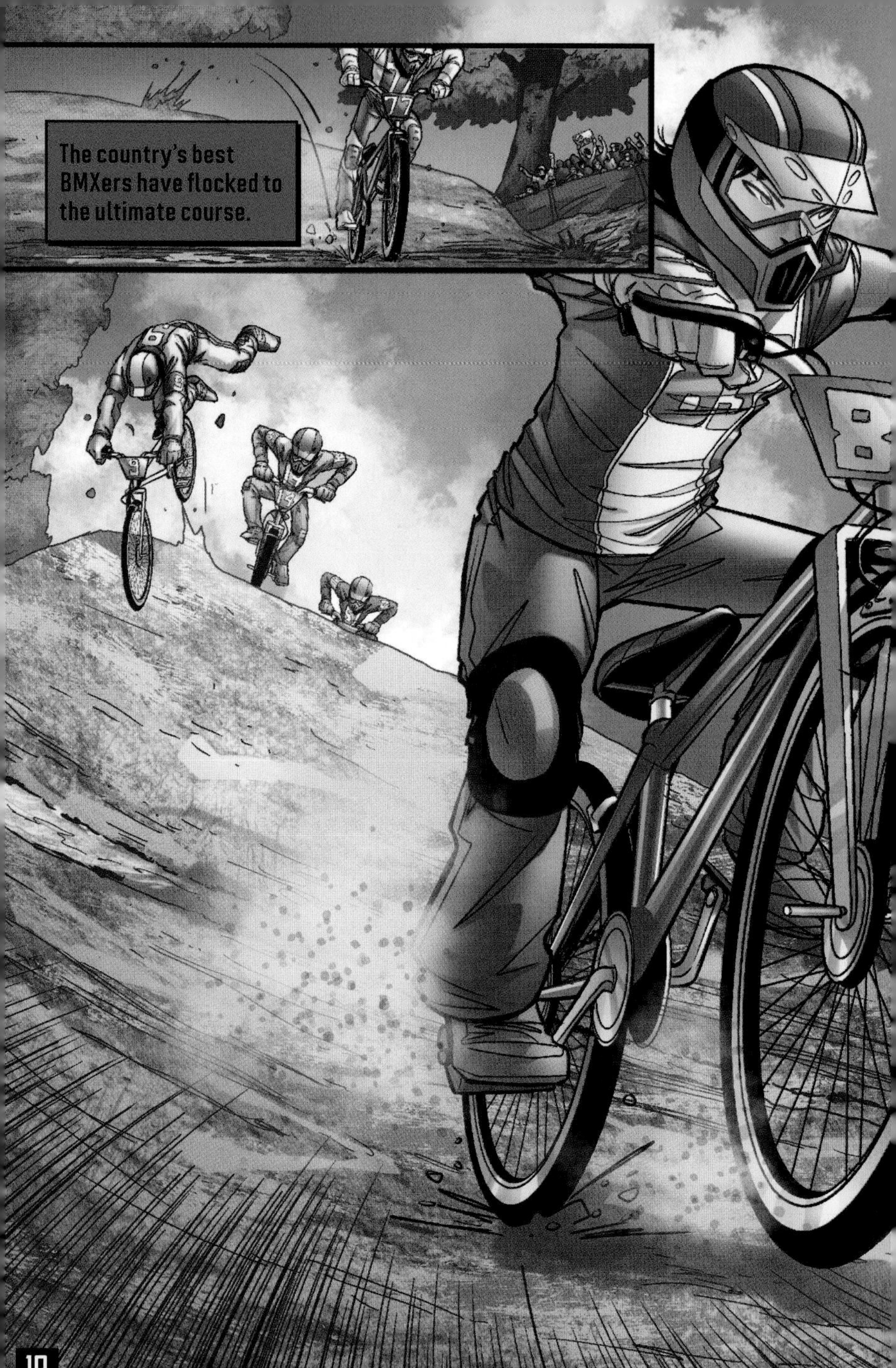
The country's best BMXers have flocked to the ultimate course.

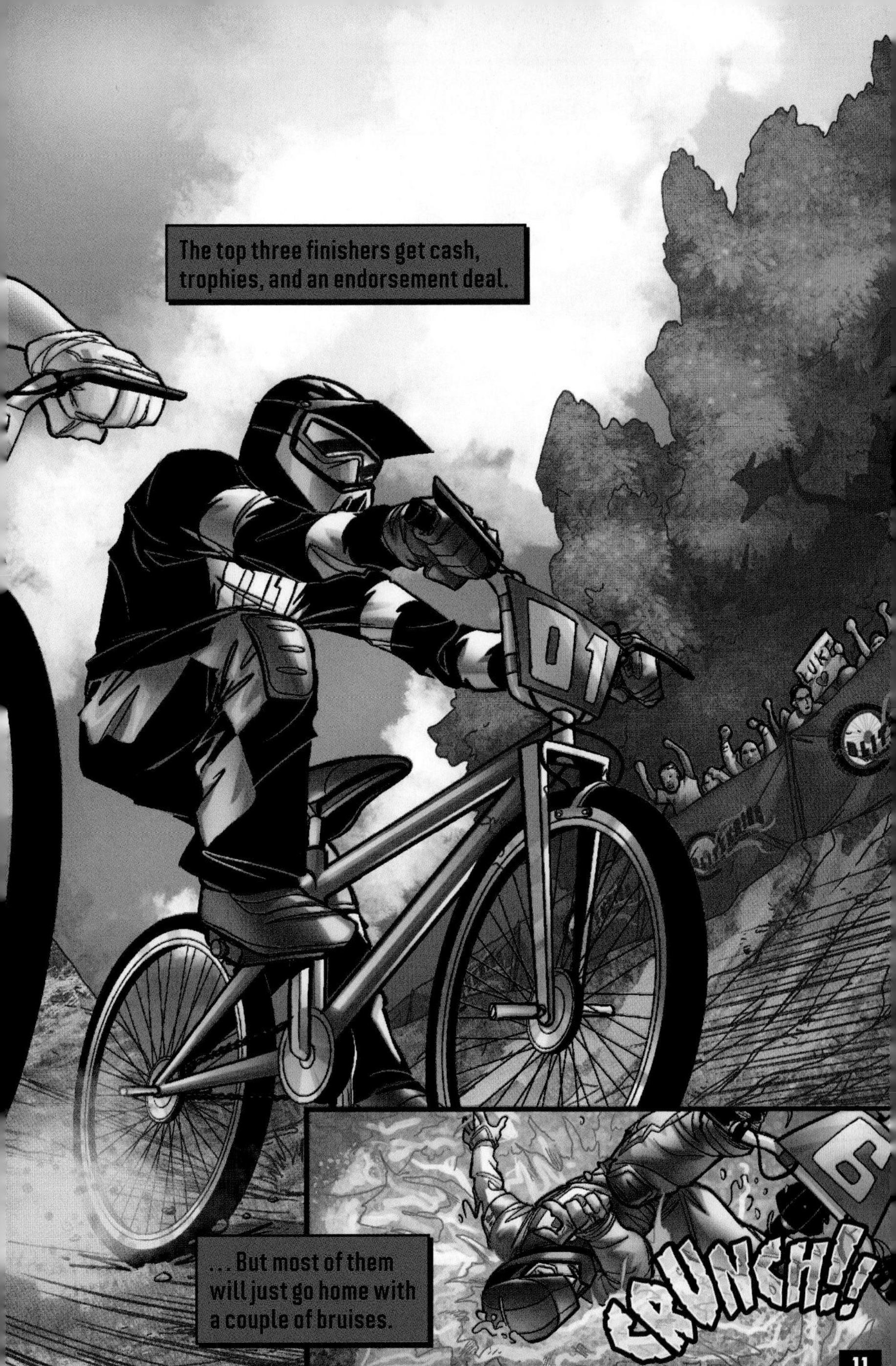

The top three finishers get cash, trophies, and an endorsement deal.
01
... But most of them will just go home with a couple of bruises.
CRUNCH!!

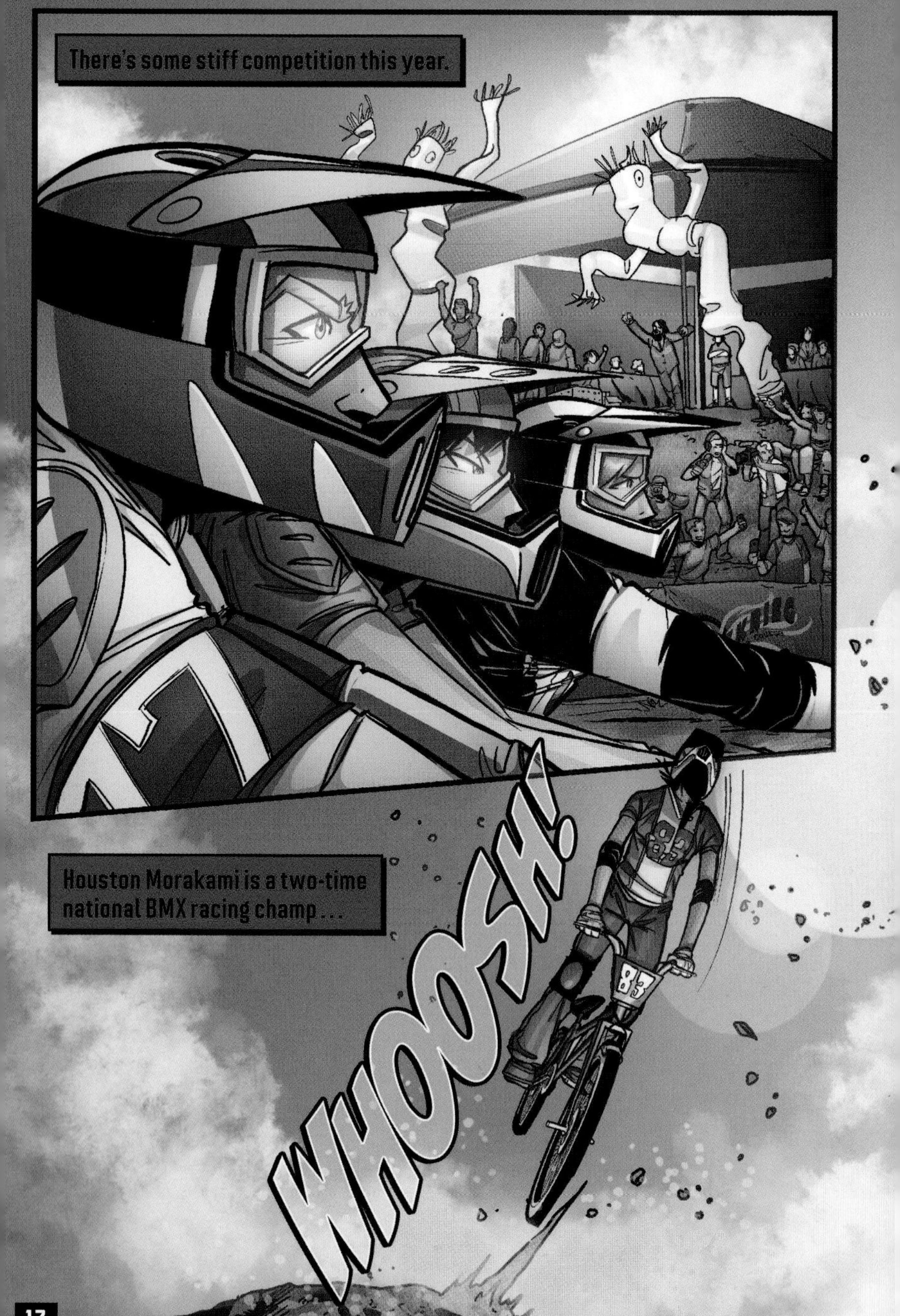
There's some stiff competition this year.
Houston Morakami is a two-time national BMX racing champ . . .
WHOOSH!

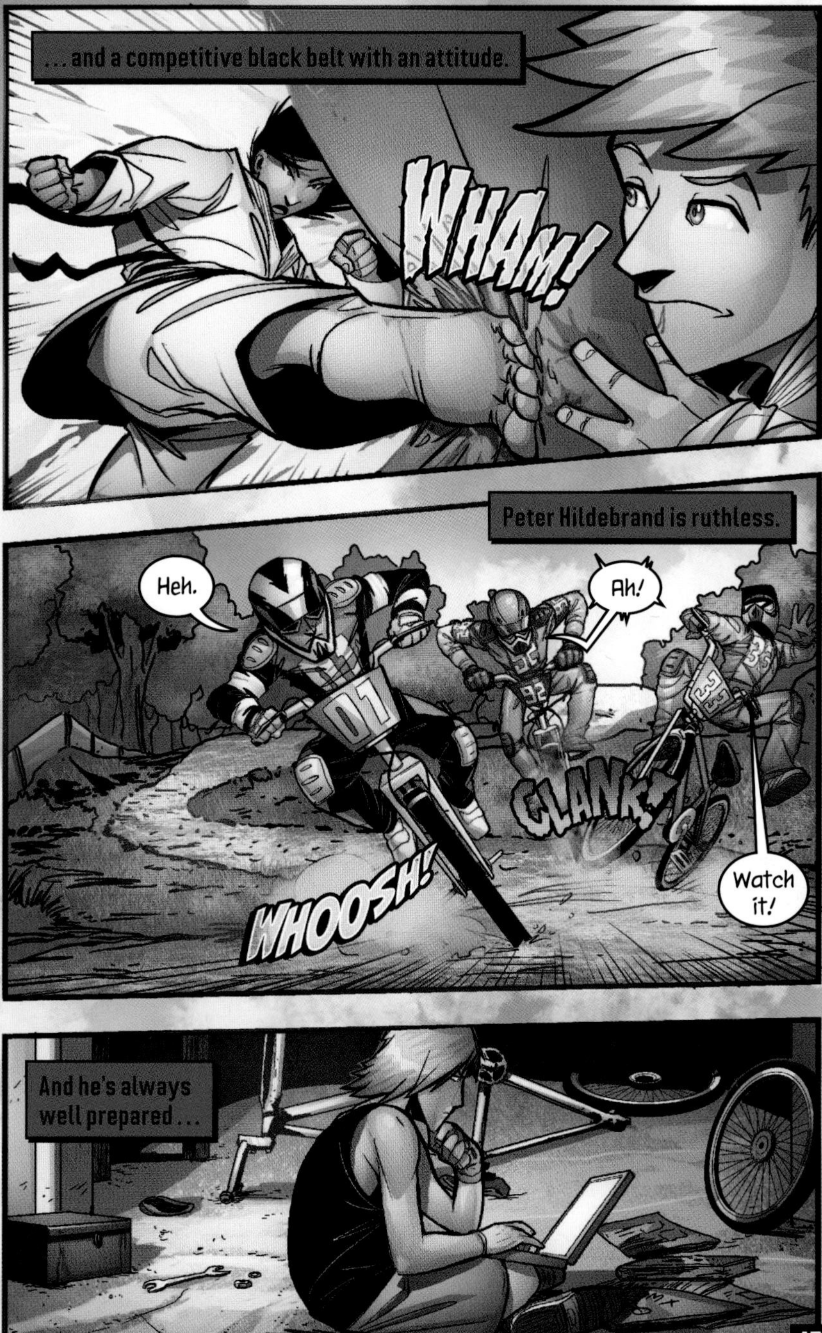

... and a competitive black belt with an attitude.
WHAM!
Peter Hildebrand is ruthless.
Heh.
Ah!
CLANK!
WHOOSH!
Watch it!
And he's always well prepared . . .

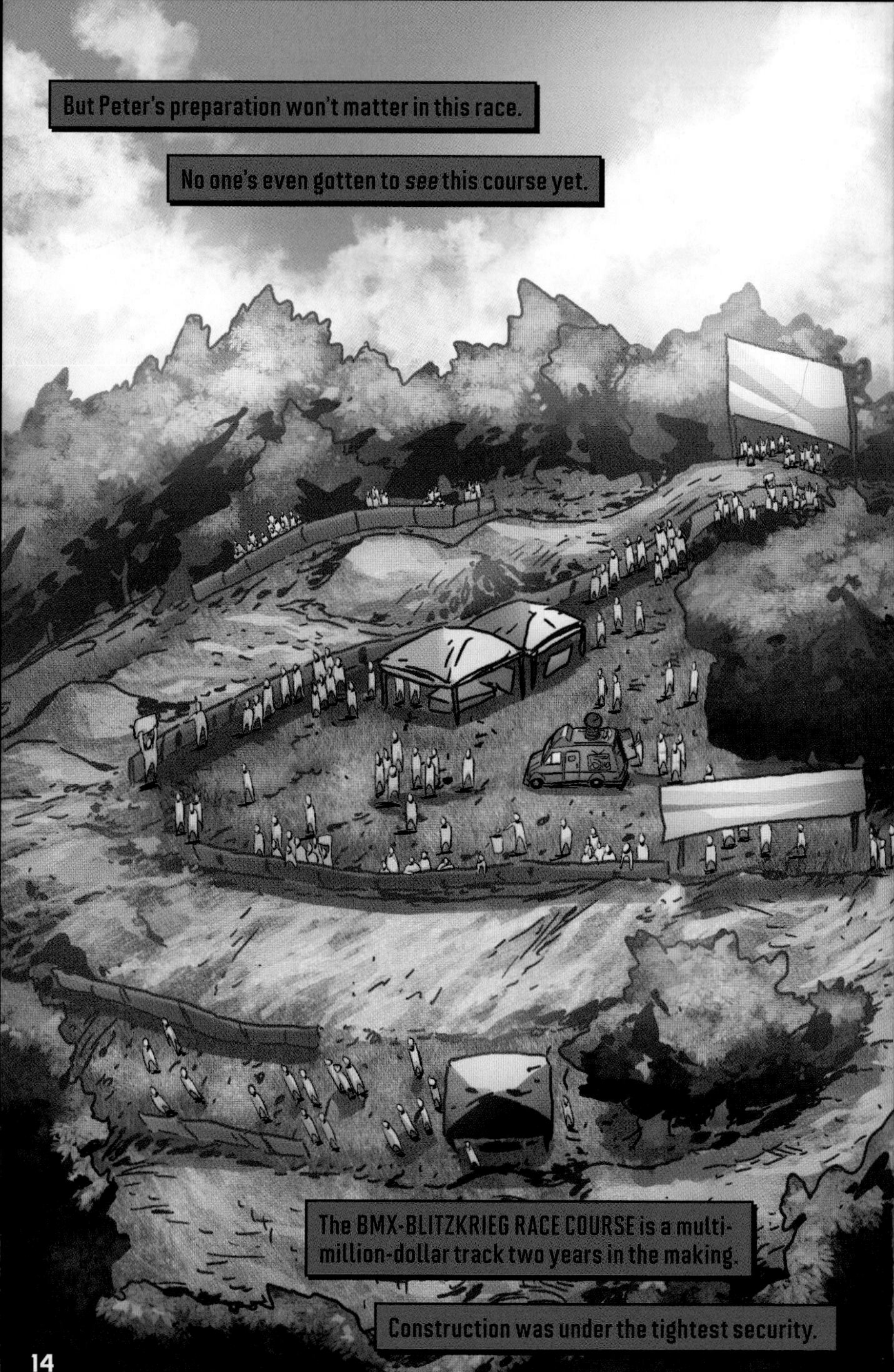
But Peter's preparation won't matter in this race.
No one's even gotten to *see* this course yet.
The BMX-BLITZKRIEG RACE COURSE is a multi-million-dollar track two years in the making.
Construction was under the tightest security.

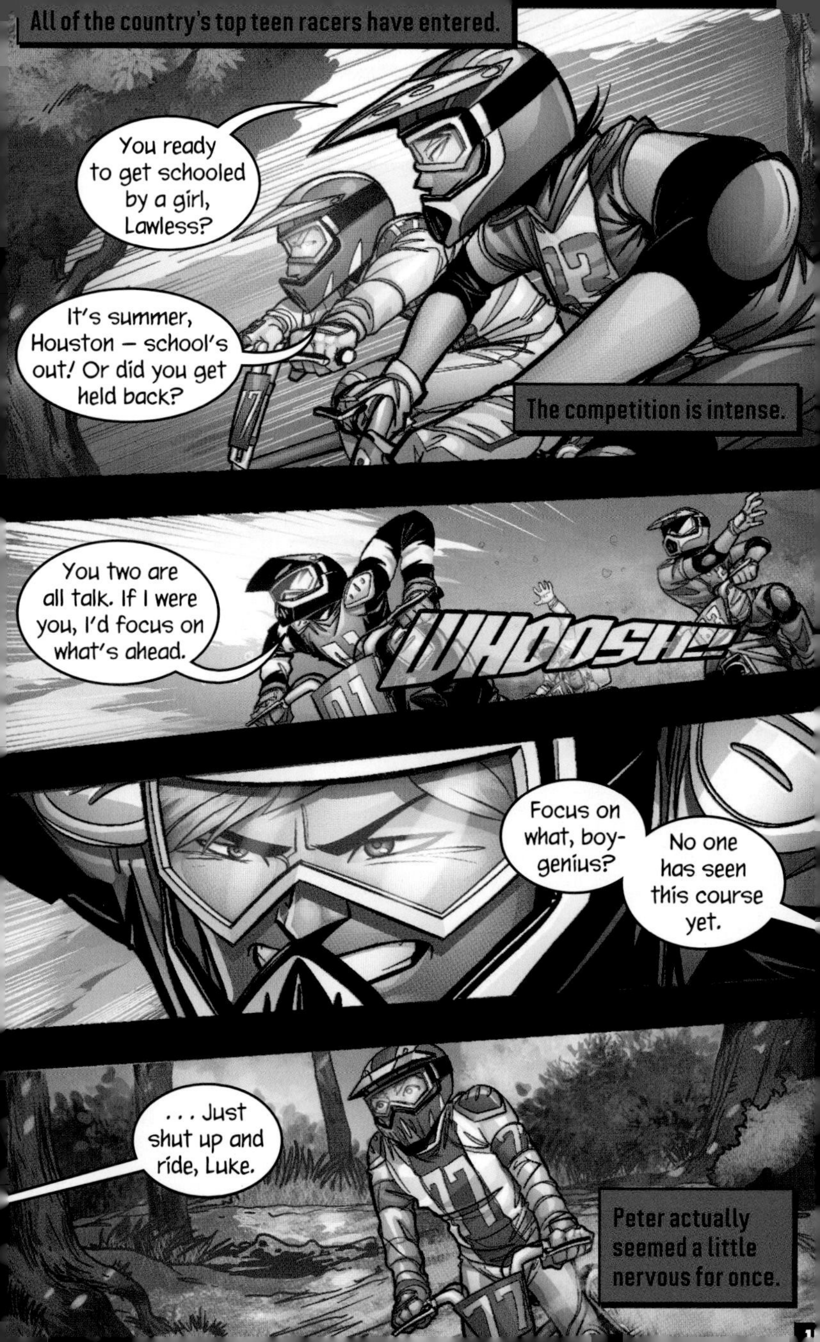
All of the country's top teen racers have entered.
You ready to get schooled by a girl, Lawless?
It's summer, Houston — school's out! Or did you get held back?
The competition is intense.
You two are all talk. If I were you, I'd focus on what's ahead.
WHOOSH!!
Focus on what, boy-genius?
No one has seen this course yet.
. . . Just shut up and ride, Luke.
Peter actually seemed a little nervous for once.

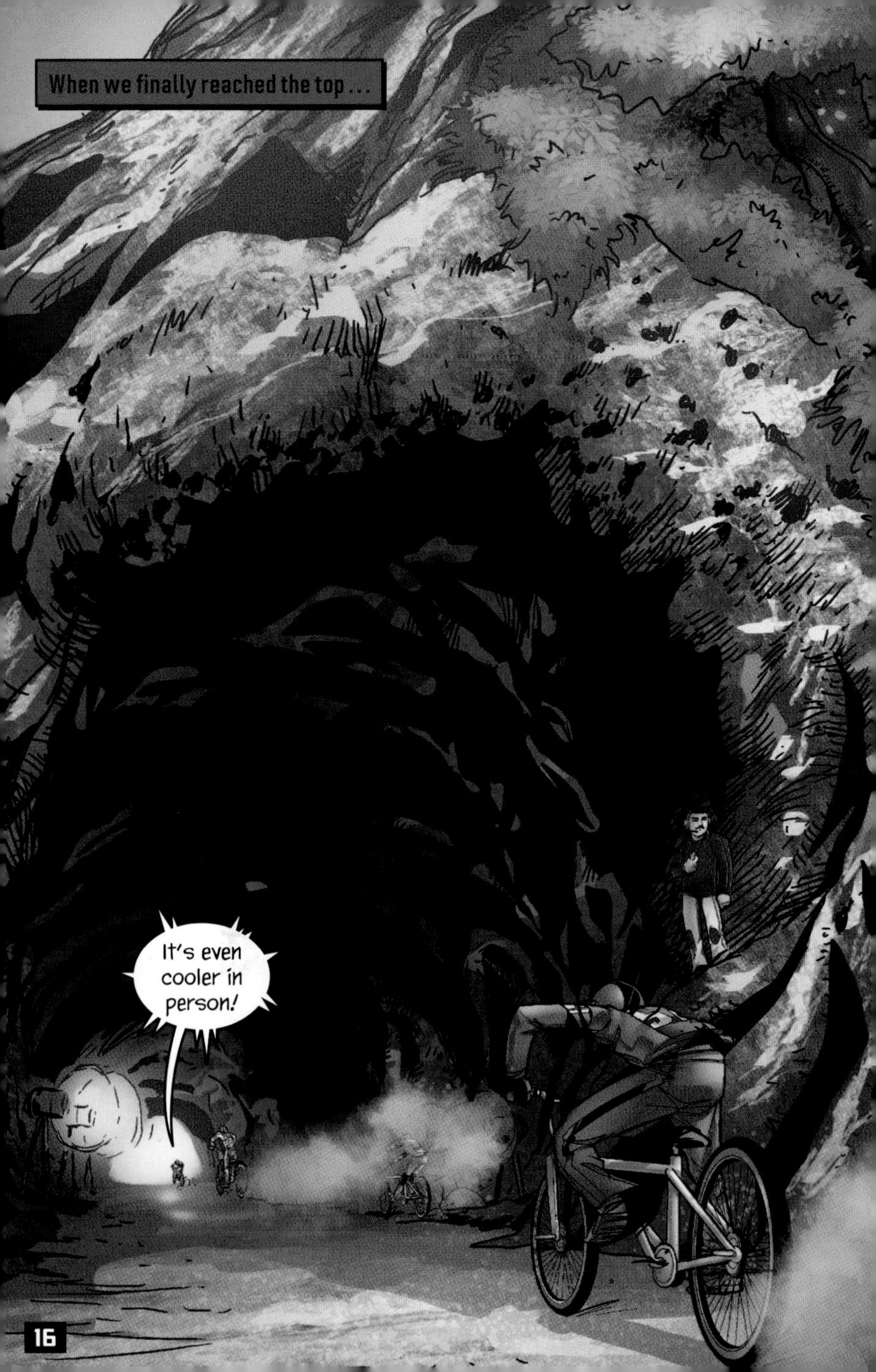
When we finally reached the top . . .
It's even cooler in person!

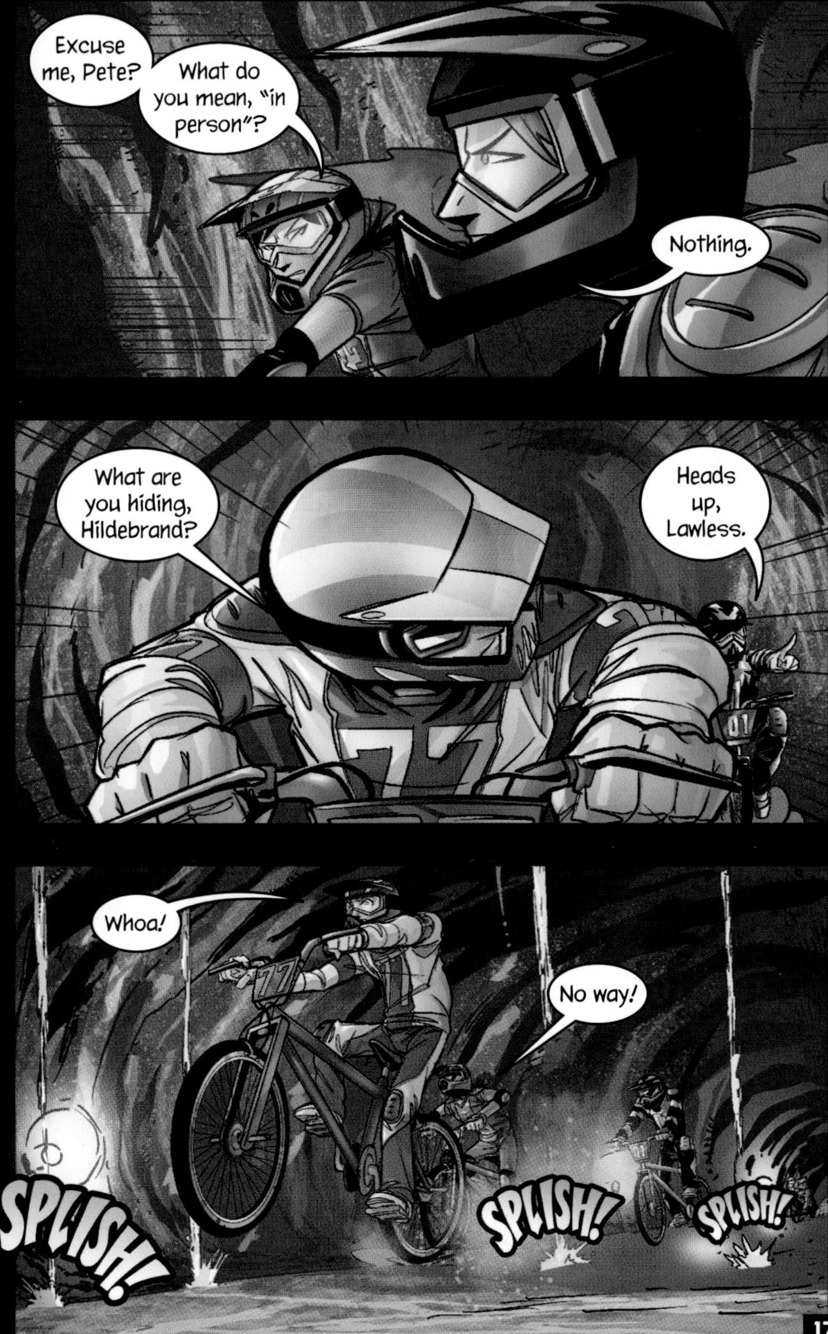
Excuse me, Pete?
What do you mean, "in person"?
Nothing.
What are you hiding, Hildebrand?
Heads up, Lawless.
Whoa!
No way!
SPLISH!
SPLISH!
SPLISH!

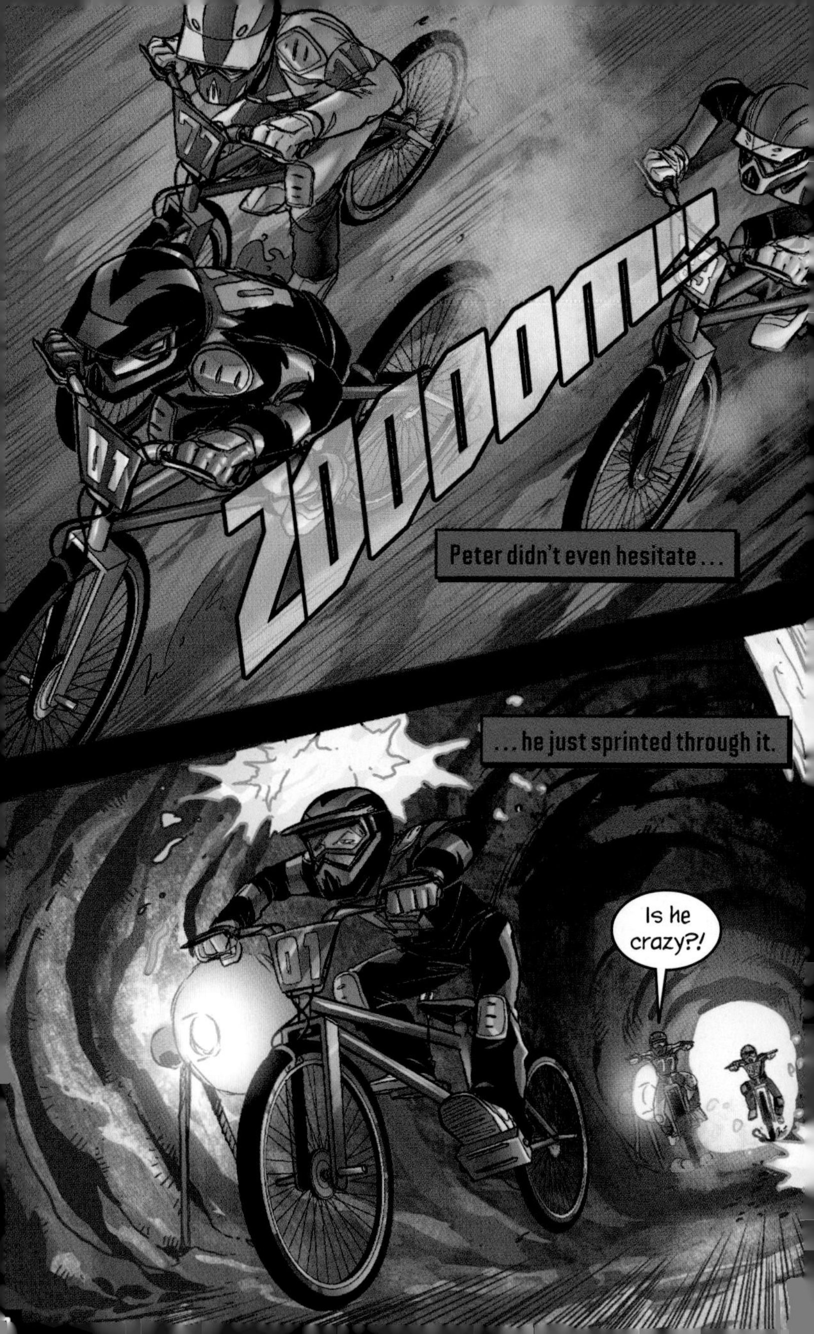
ZOOOOM!!
Peter didn't even hesitate . . .
. . . he just sprinted through it.
Is he crazy?!

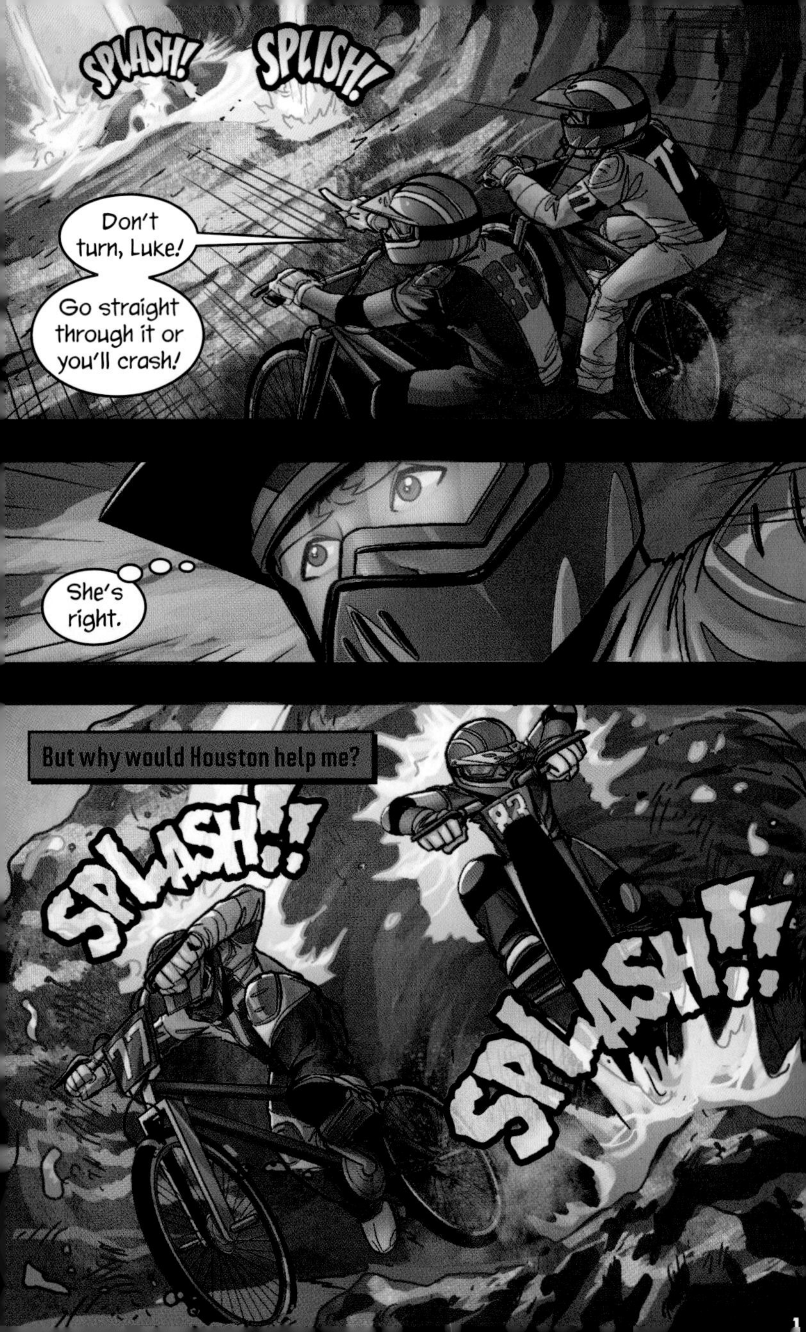
SPLASH!
SPLISH!
Don't turn, Luke!
Go straight through it or you'll crash!
She's right.
But why would Houston help me?
SPLASH!!
SPLASH!!

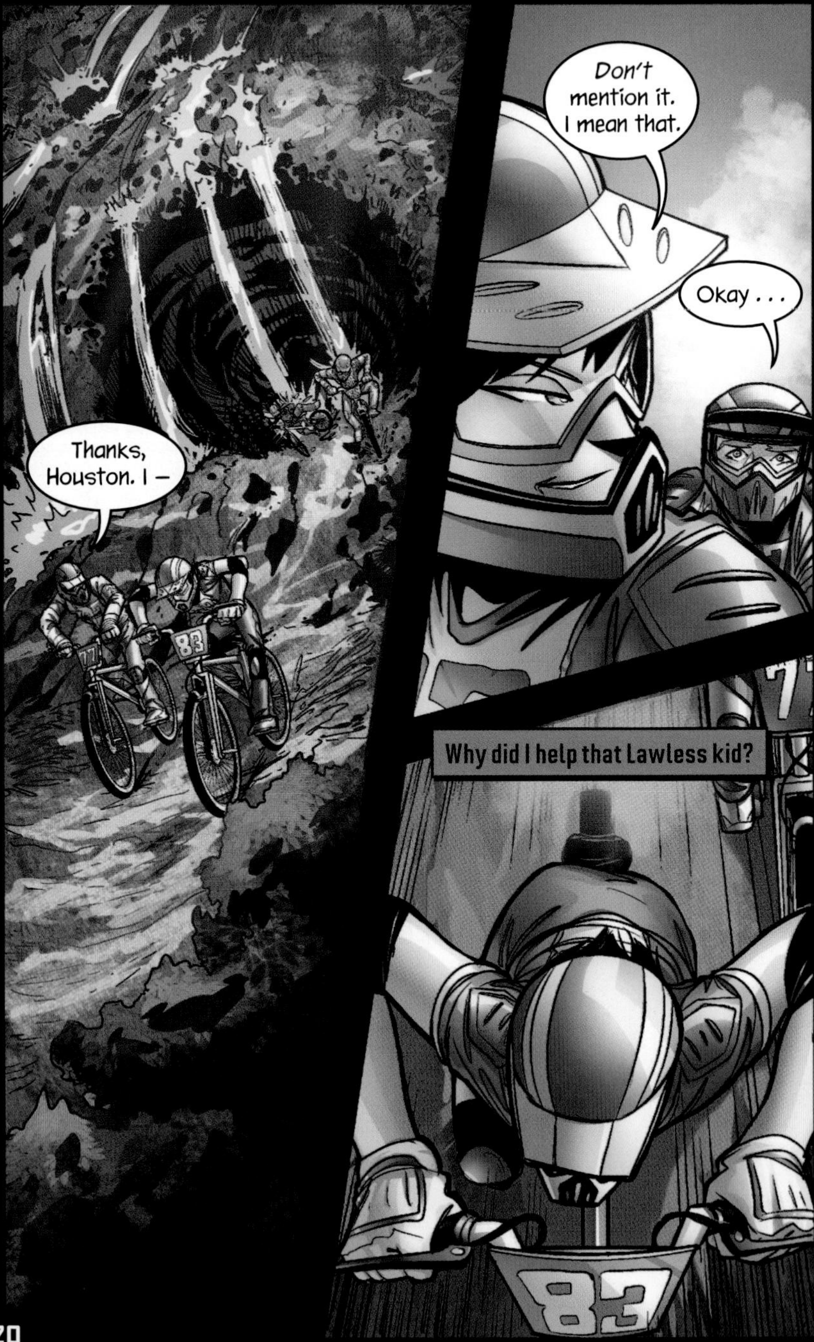
Thanks, Houston. I –
Don't mention it. I mean that.
Okay . . .
Why did I help that Lawless kid?

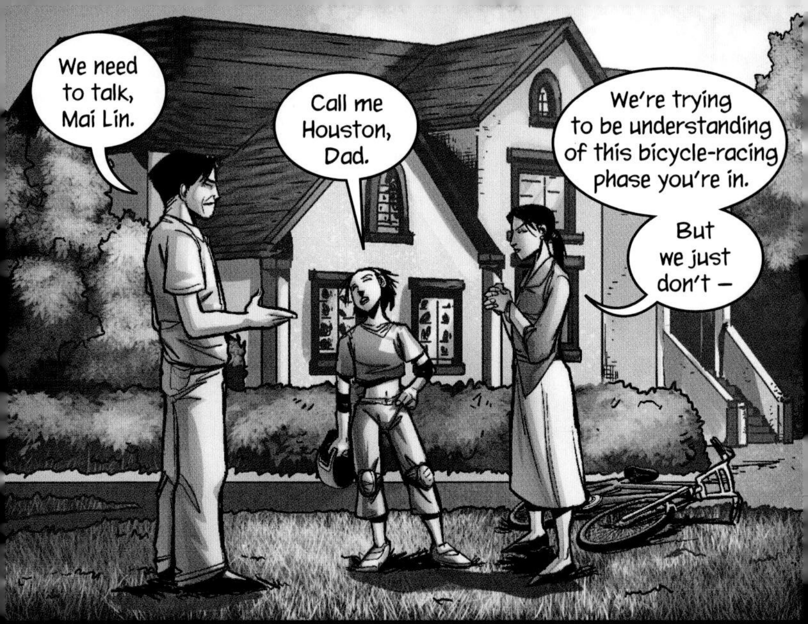
We need to talk, Mai Lin.
Call me Houston, Dad.
We're trying to be understanding of this bicycle-racing phase you're in.
But we just don't –

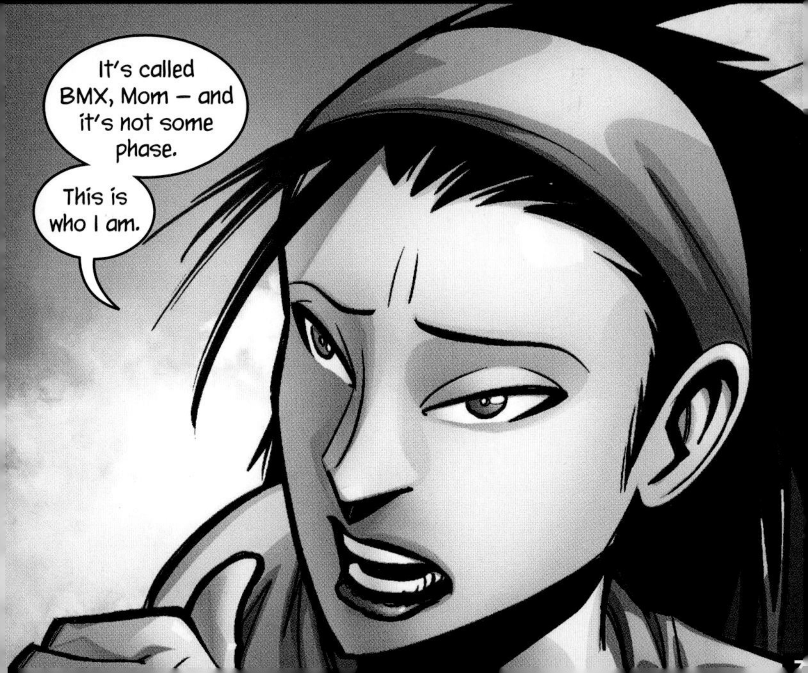
It's called BMX, Mom – and it's not some phase.
This is who I am.

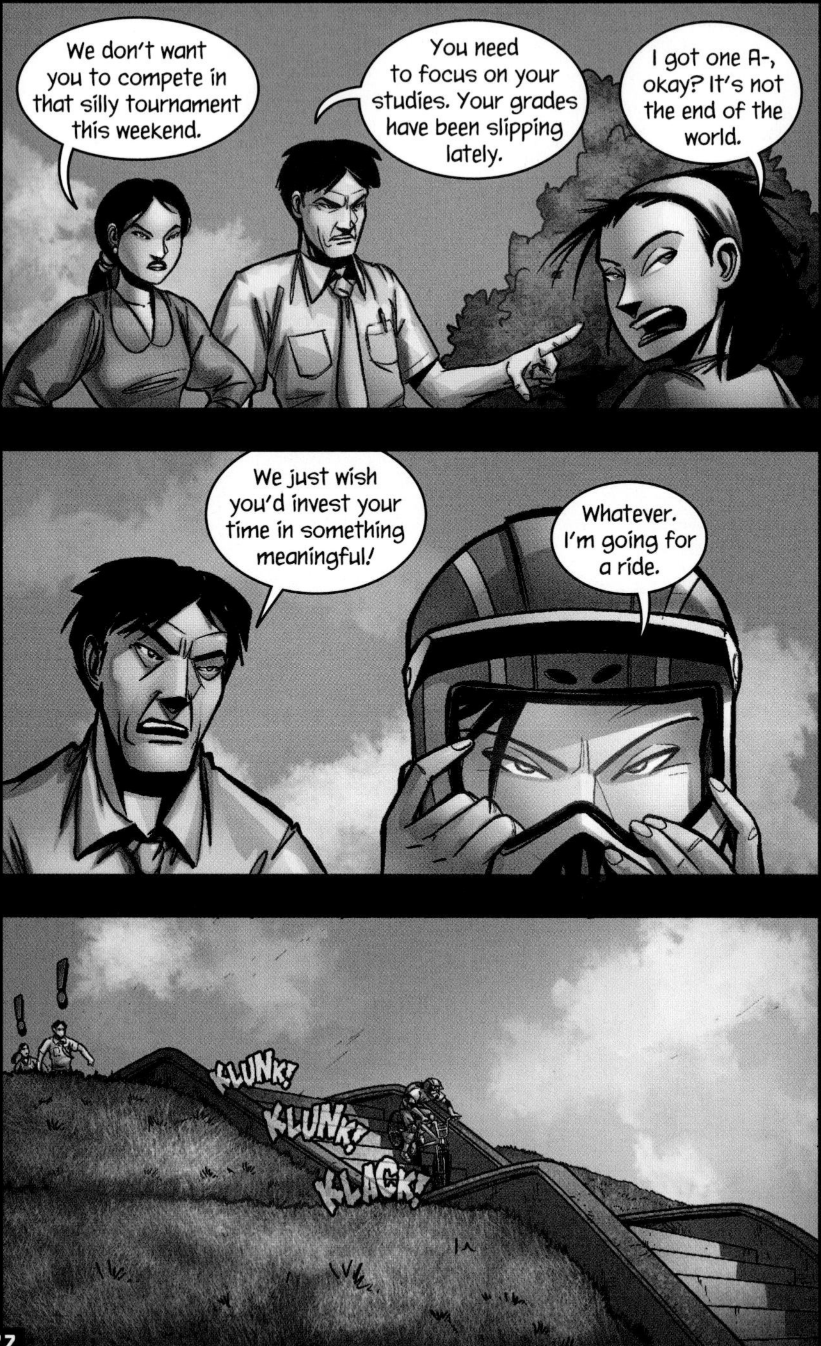
We don't want you to compete in that silly tournament this weekend.
You need to focus on your studies. Your grades have been slipping lately.
I got one A-, okay? It's not the end of the world.
We just wish you'd invest your time in something meaningful!
Whatever. I'm going for a ride.
!
!
KLUNK!
KLUNK!
KLACK!

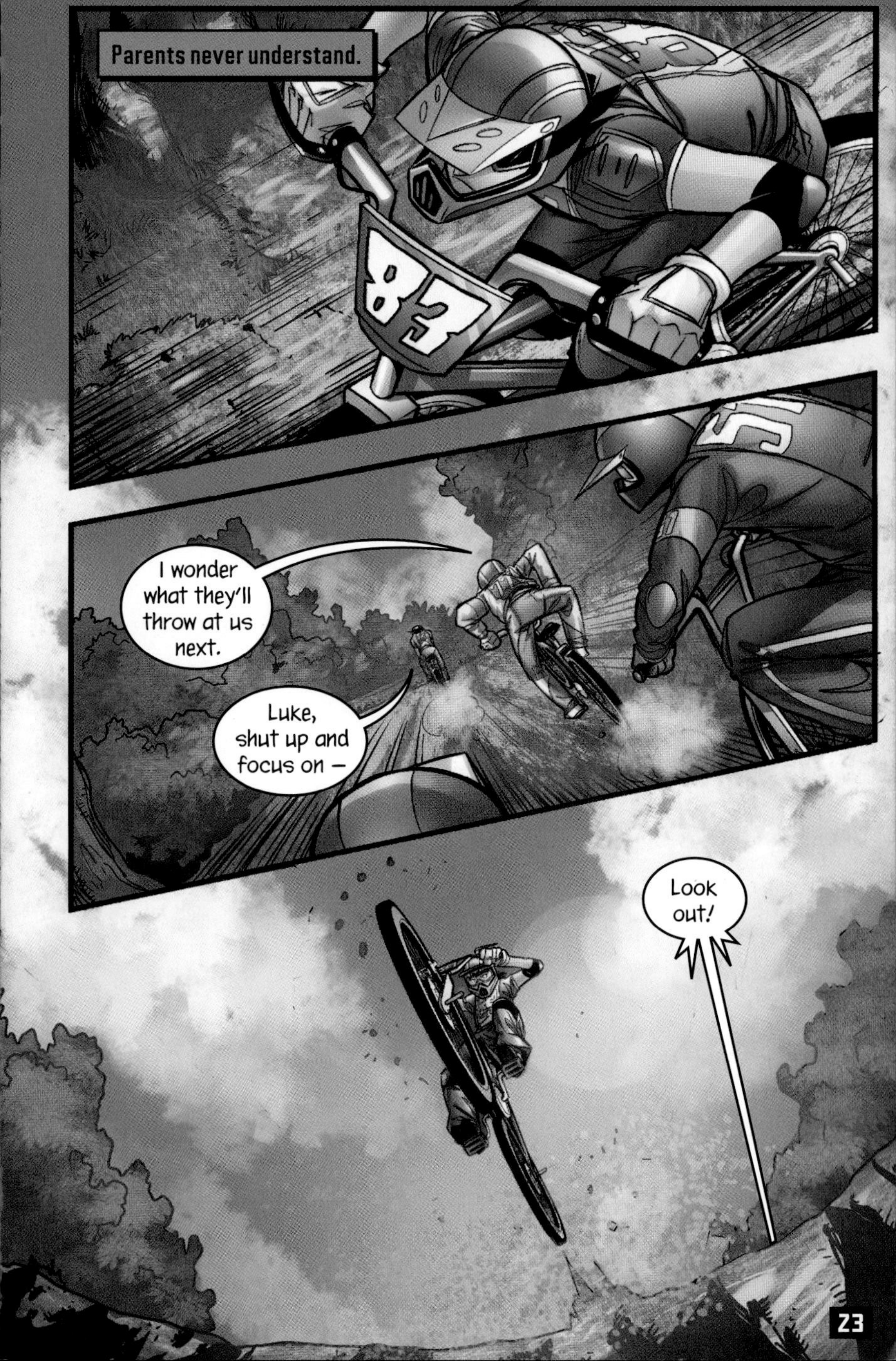
Parents never understand.
I wonder what they'll throw at us next.
Luke, shut up and focus on —
Look out!

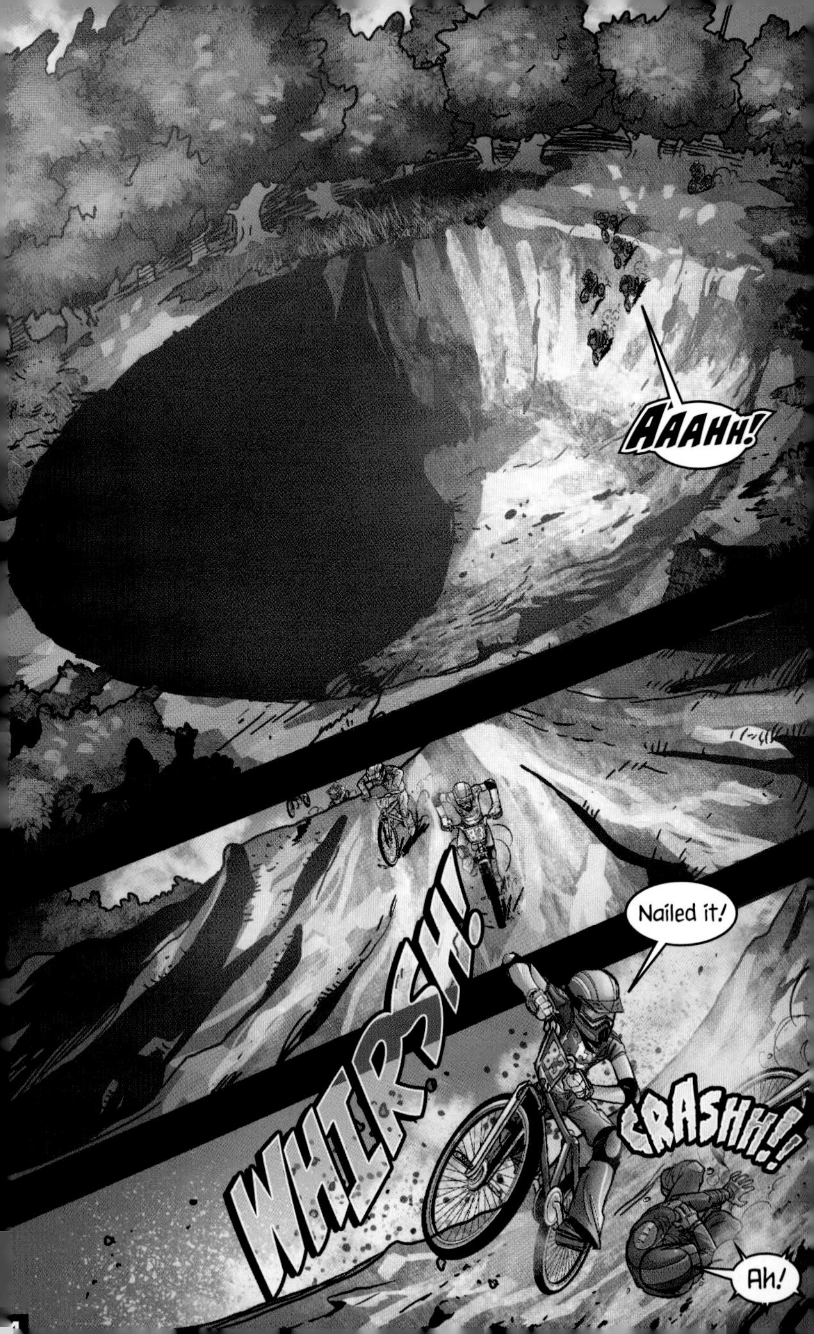
AAAHH!
WHIRSH!
Nailed it!
CRASHH!
Ah!

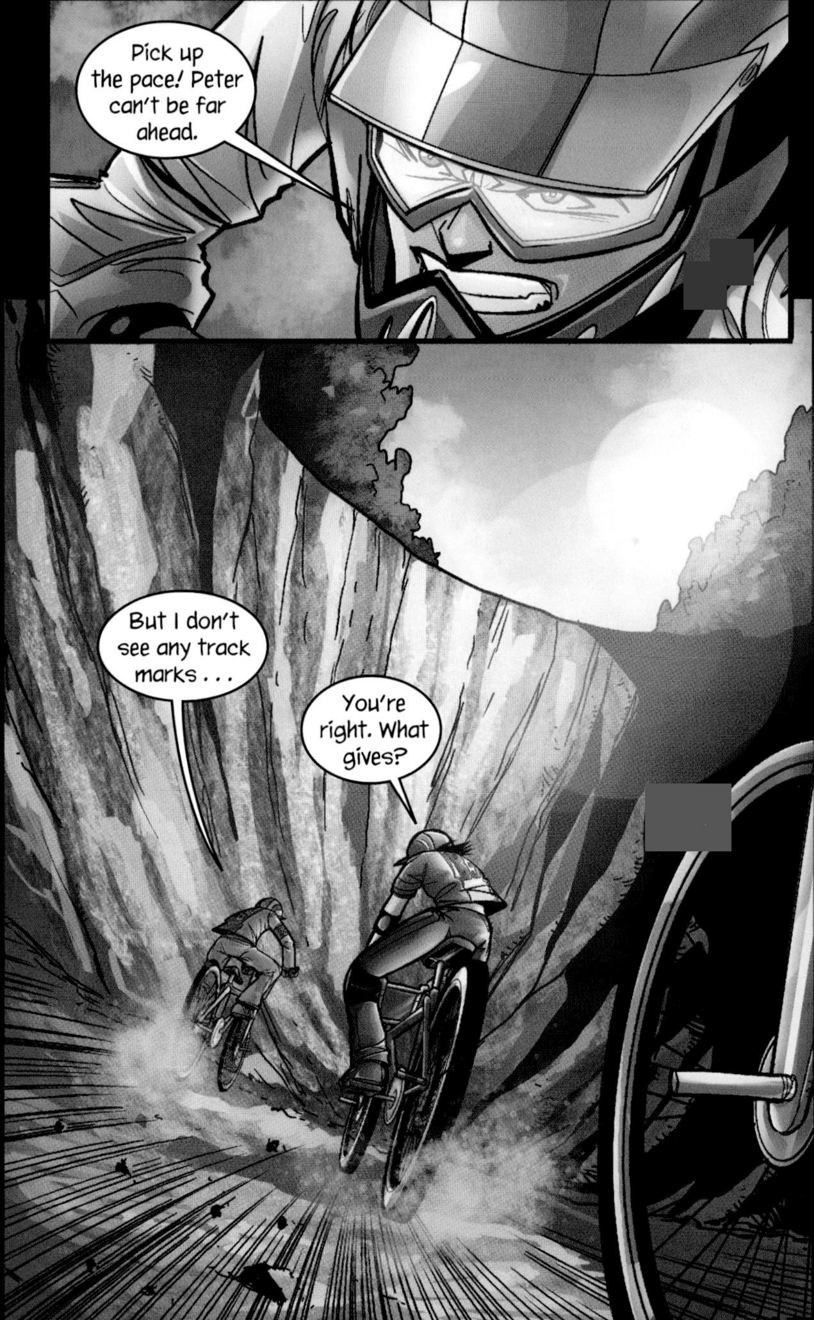
Pick up the pace! Peter can't be far ahead.
But I don't see any track marks . . .
You're right. What gives?

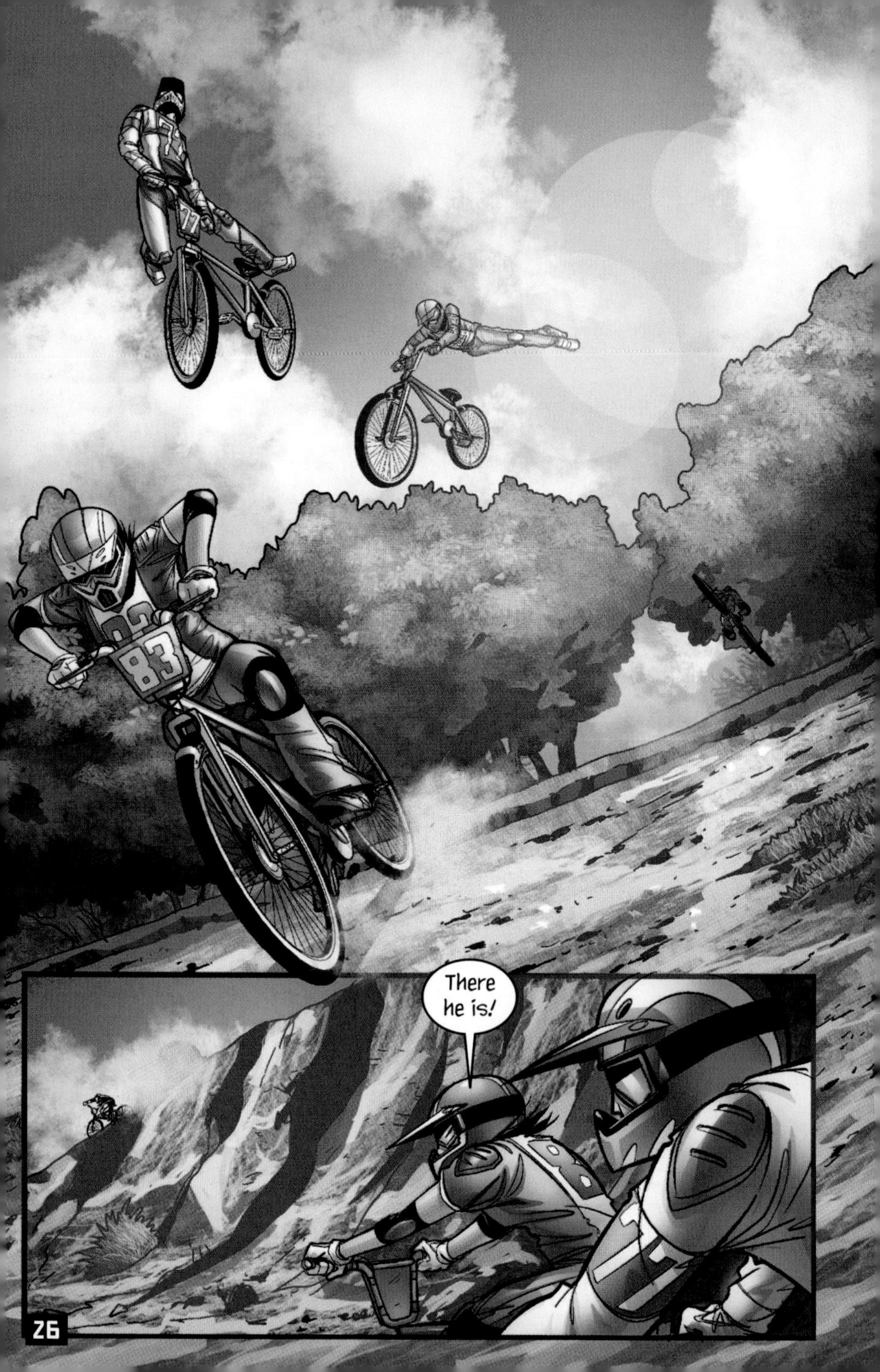
There he is!

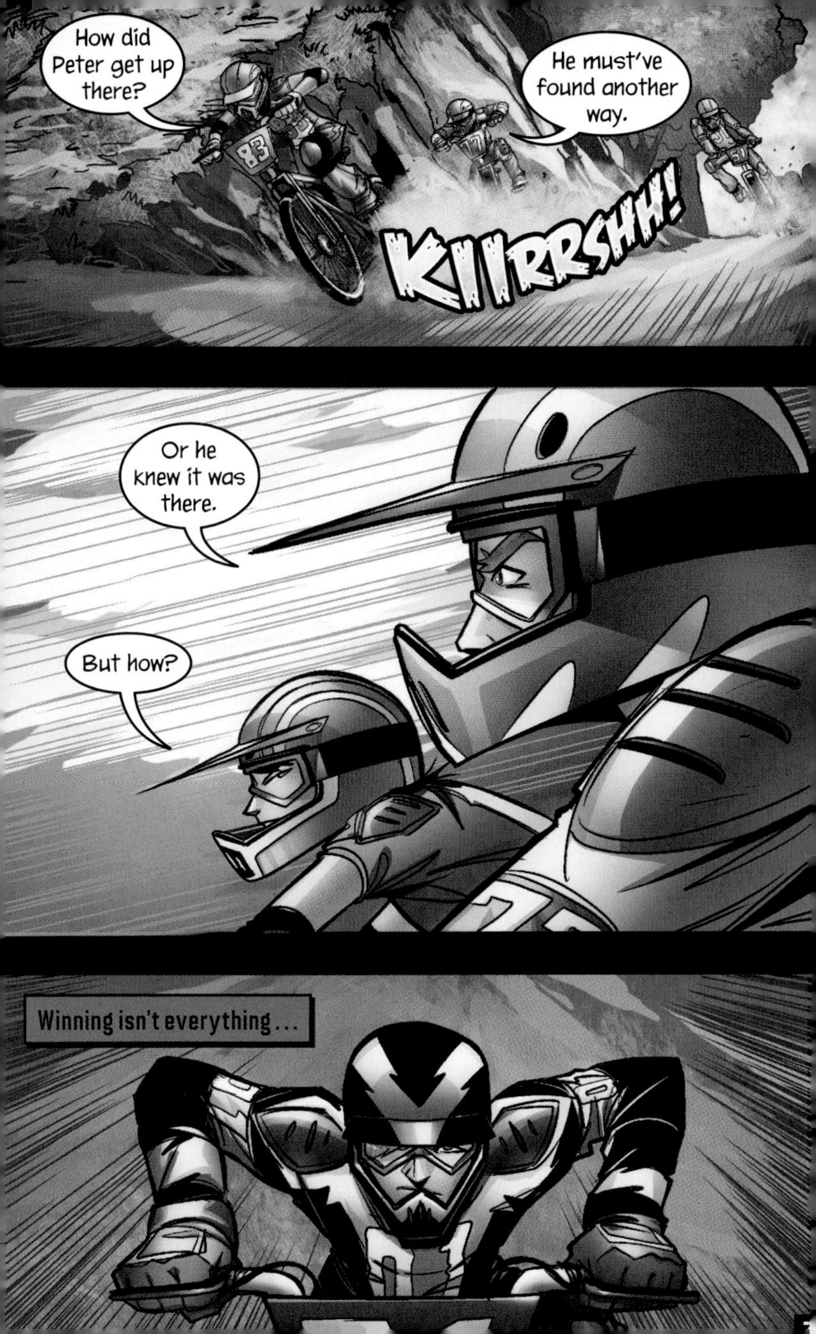
How did Peter get up there?
He must've found another way.
KIIRRSHH!
Or he knew it was there.
But how?
Winning isn't everything . . .

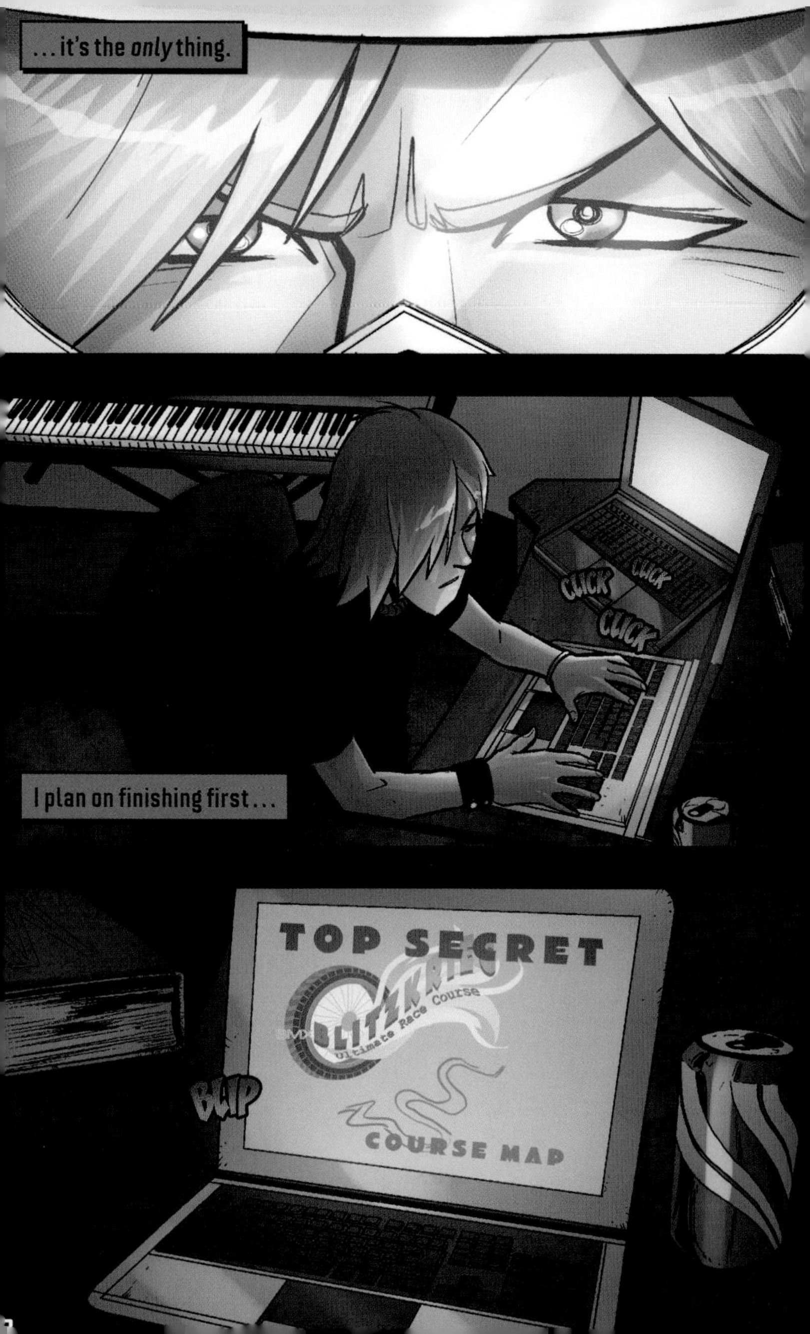
. . . it's the *only* thing.
CLICK
CLICK
CLICK
I plan on finishing first . . .
TOP SECRET
Ultimate Race Course
BLIP
COURSE MAP

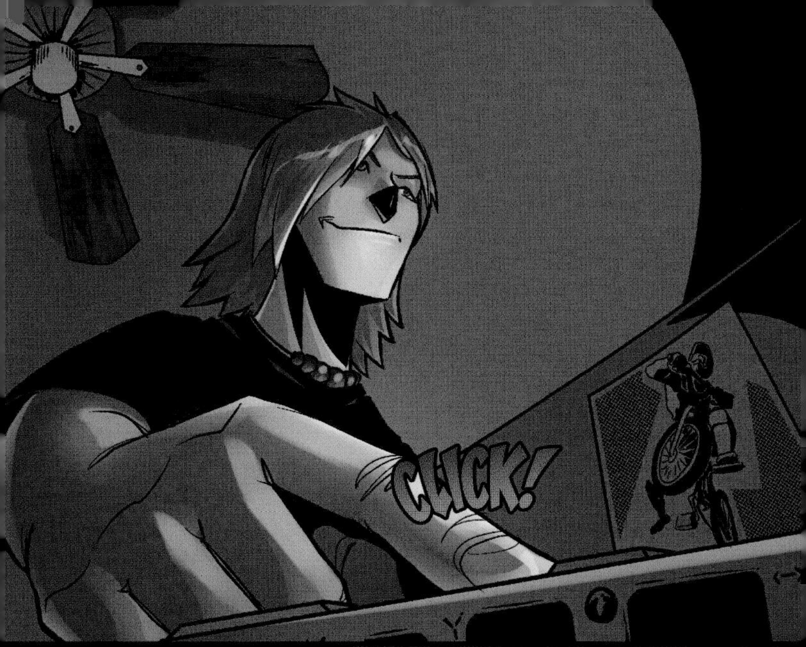
CLICK!
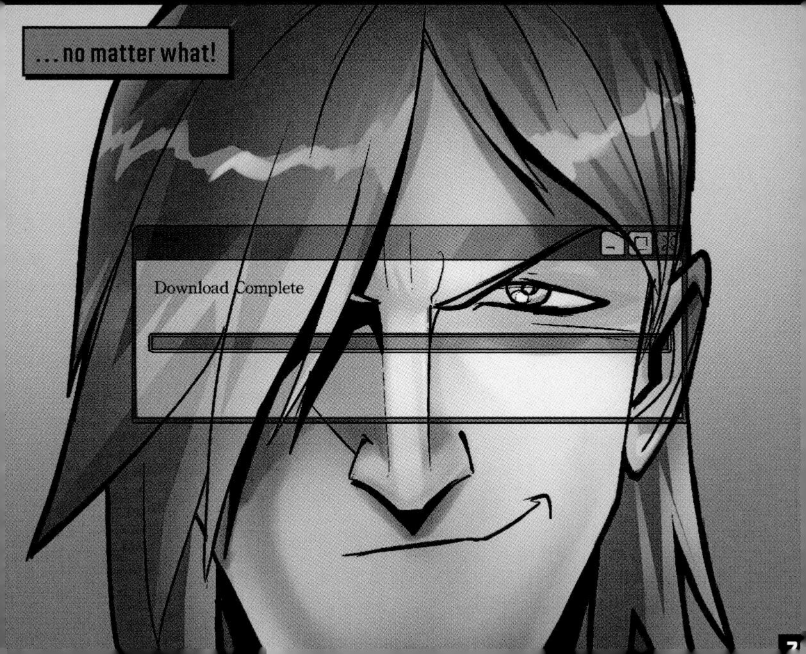
...no matter what!
Download Complete

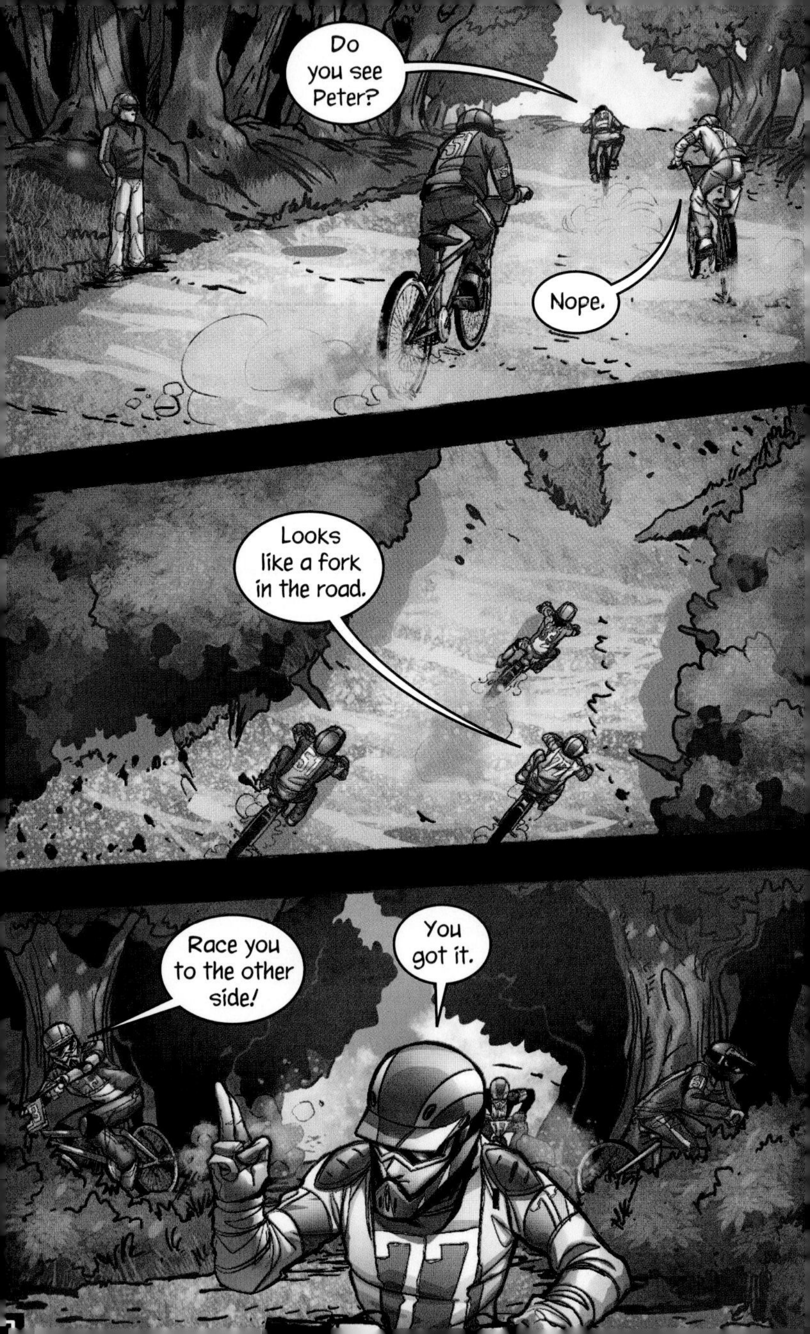
Do you see Peter?
Nope.
Looks like a fork in the road.
Race you to the other side!
You got it.

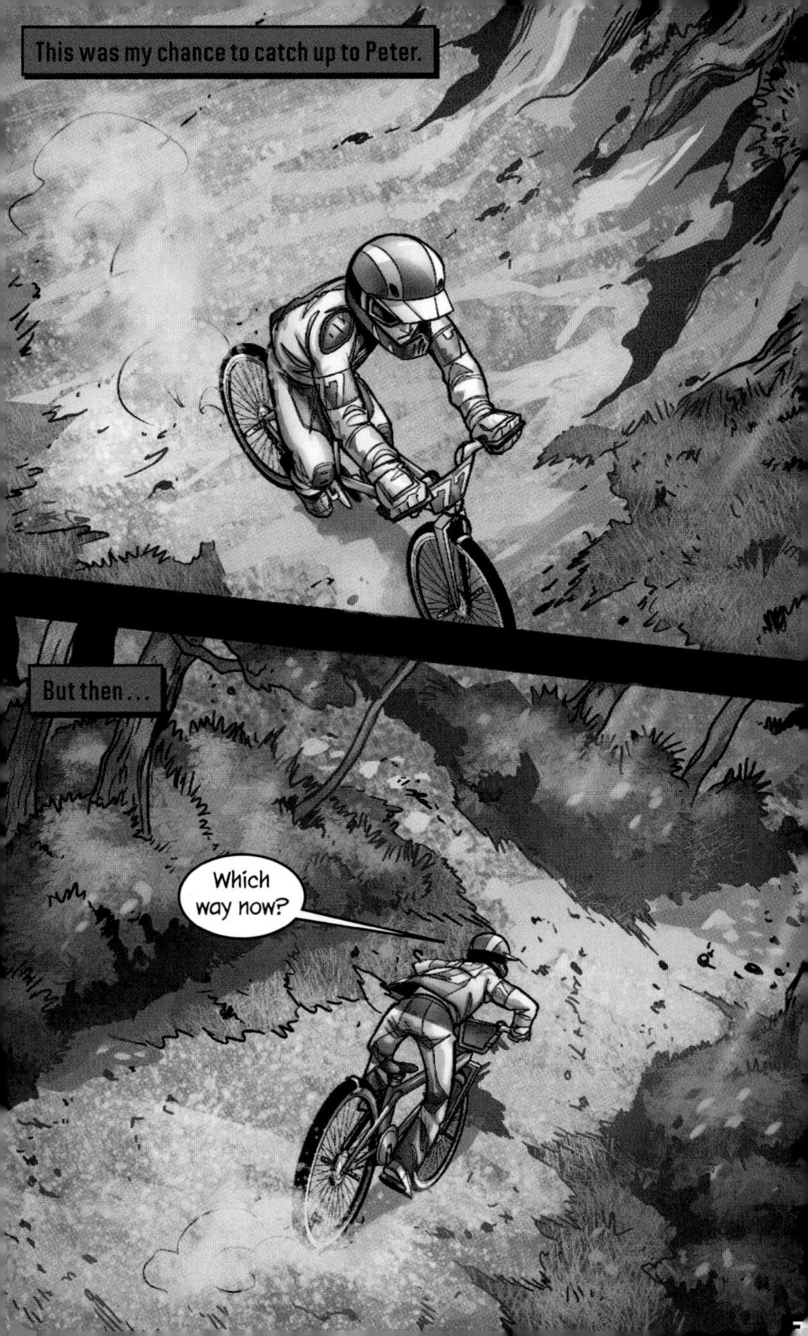
This was my chance to catch up to Peter.
But then . . .
Which way now?

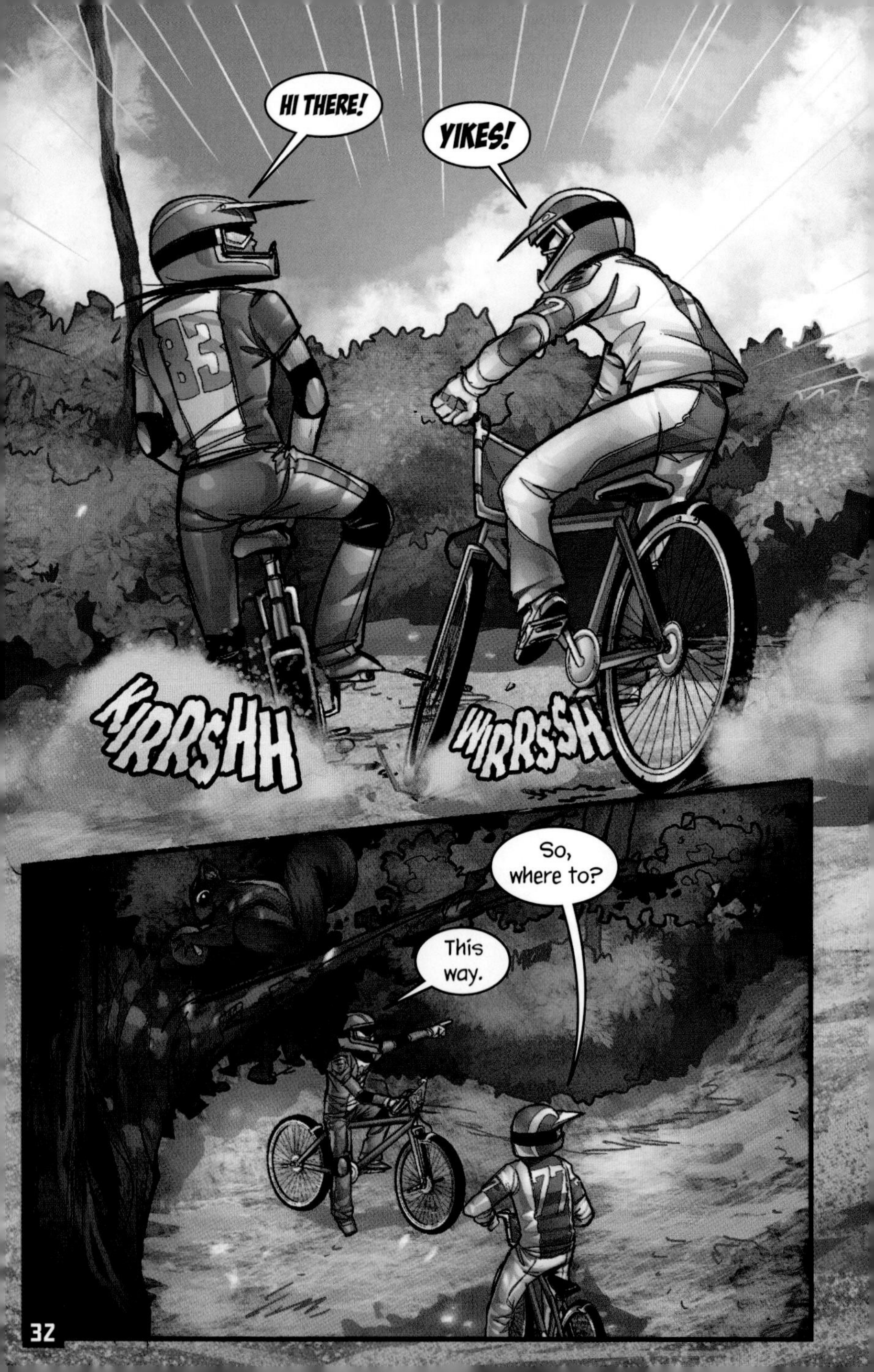
HI THERE!
YIKES!
KIRRSHH
WIRRSSH
So, where to?
This way.

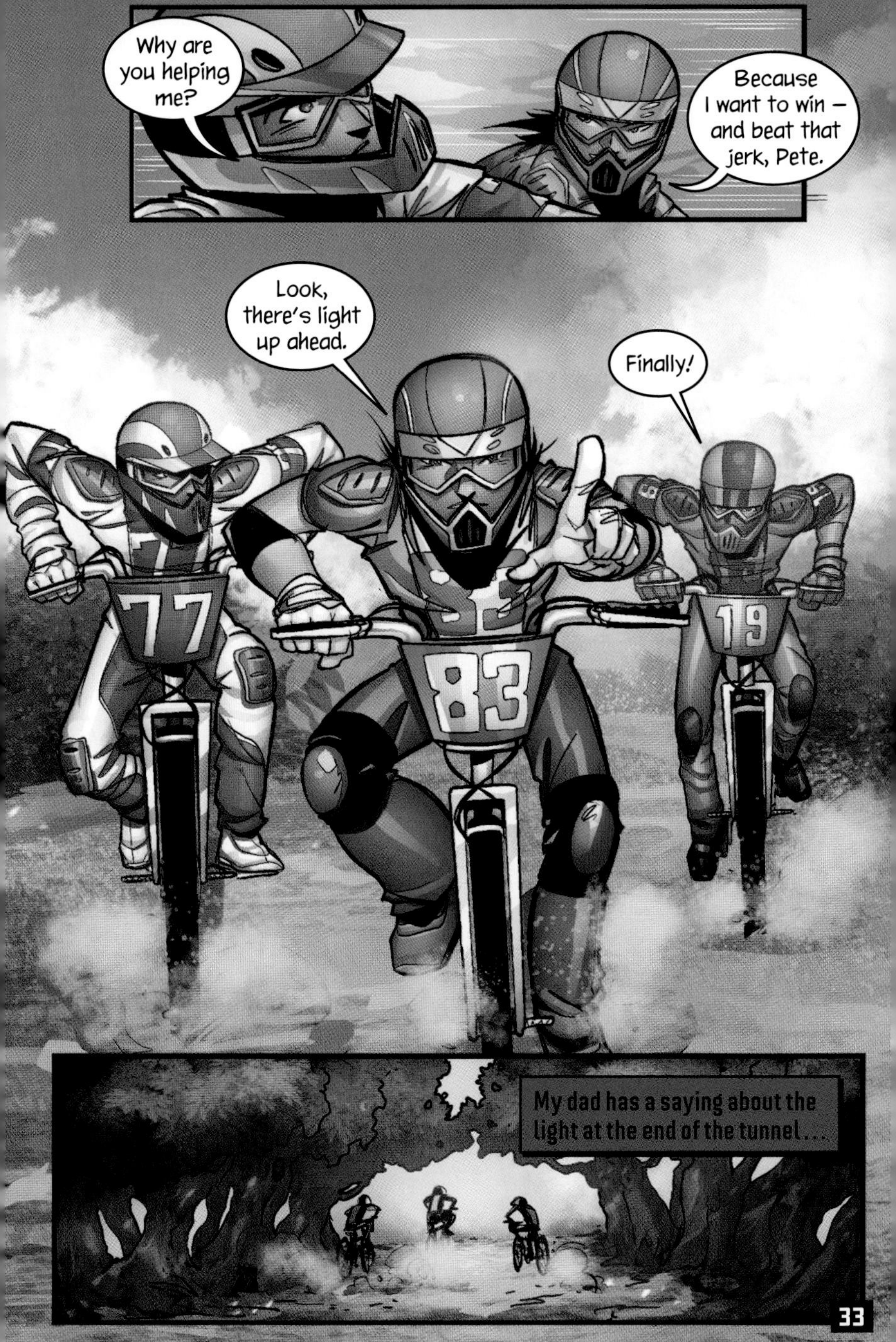

Why are you helping me?
Because I want to win — and beat that jerk, Pete.
Look, there's light up ahead.
Finally!
77
83
19
My dad has a saying about the light at the end of the tunnel . . .

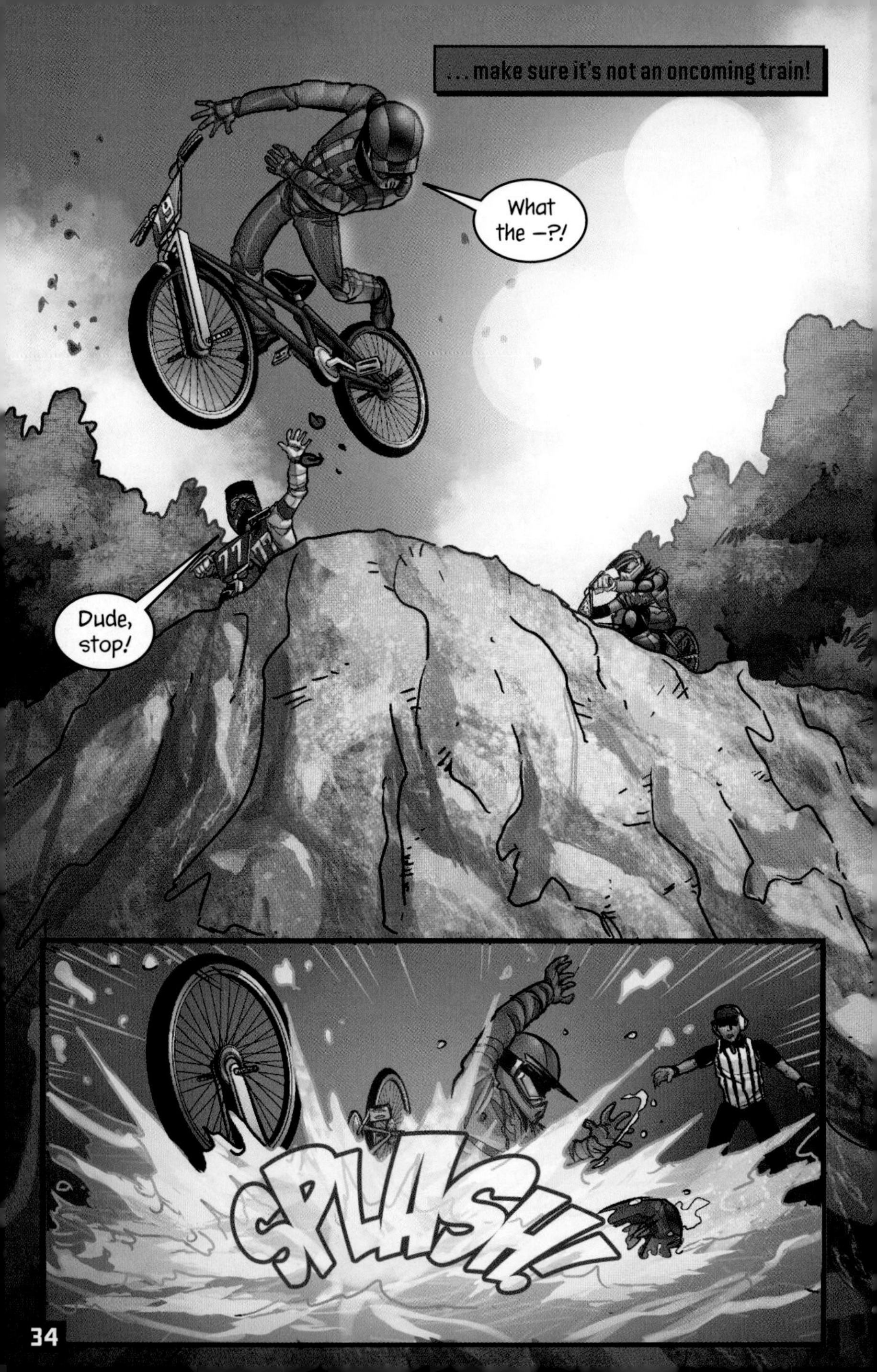
. . . make sure it's not an oncoming train!
What the –?!
Dude, stop!
SPLASH!

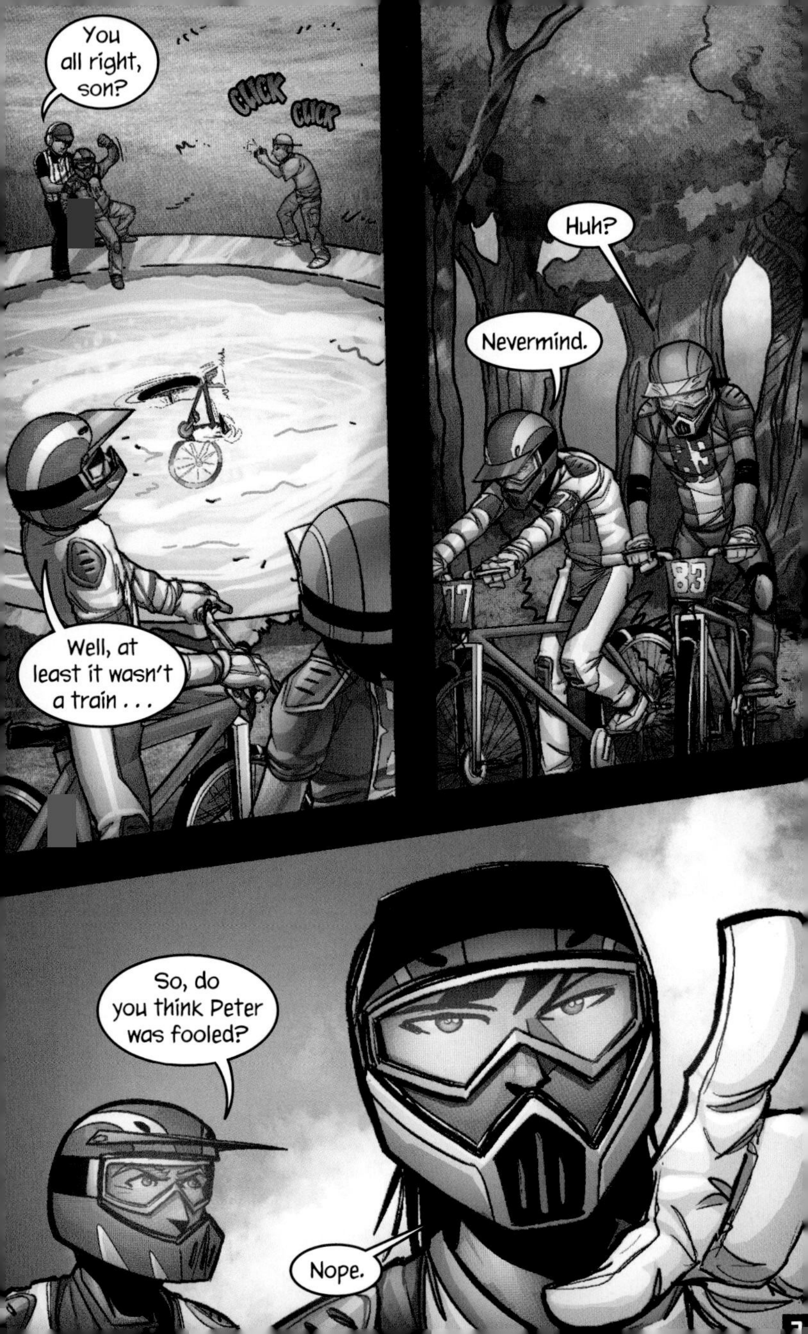
You all right, son?
CLICK
CLICK
Well, at least it wasn't a train . . .
Huh?
Nevermind.
77
83
So, do you think Peter was fooled?
Nope.

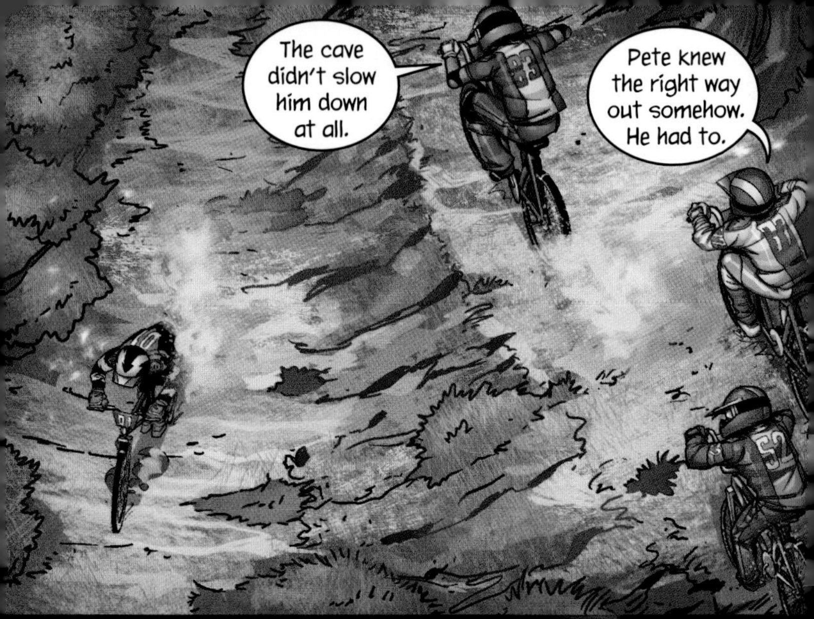
The cave didn't slow him down at all.
Pete knew the right way out somehow. He had to.

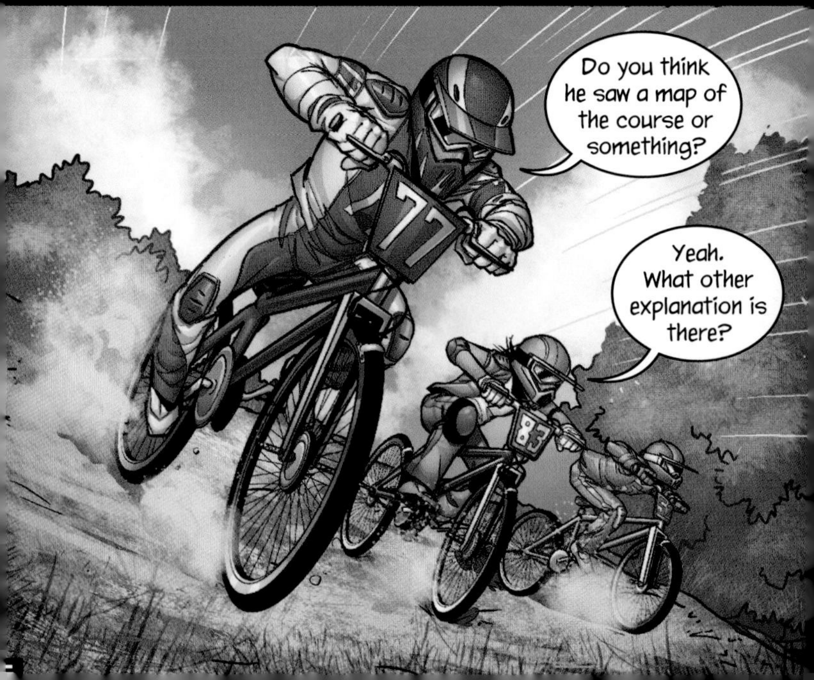
Do you think he saw a map of the course or something?
Yeah. What other explanation is there?

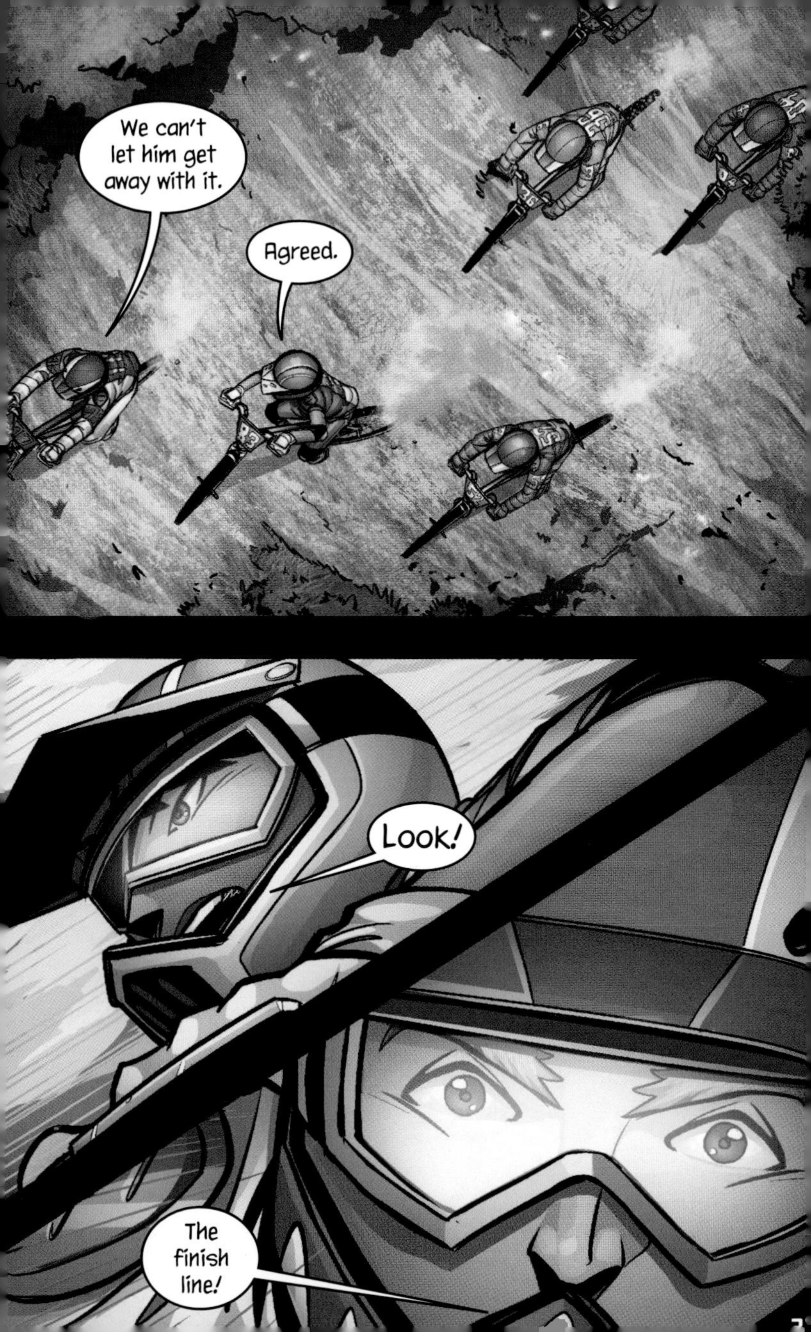
We can't let him get away with it.
Agreed.
Look!
The finish line!

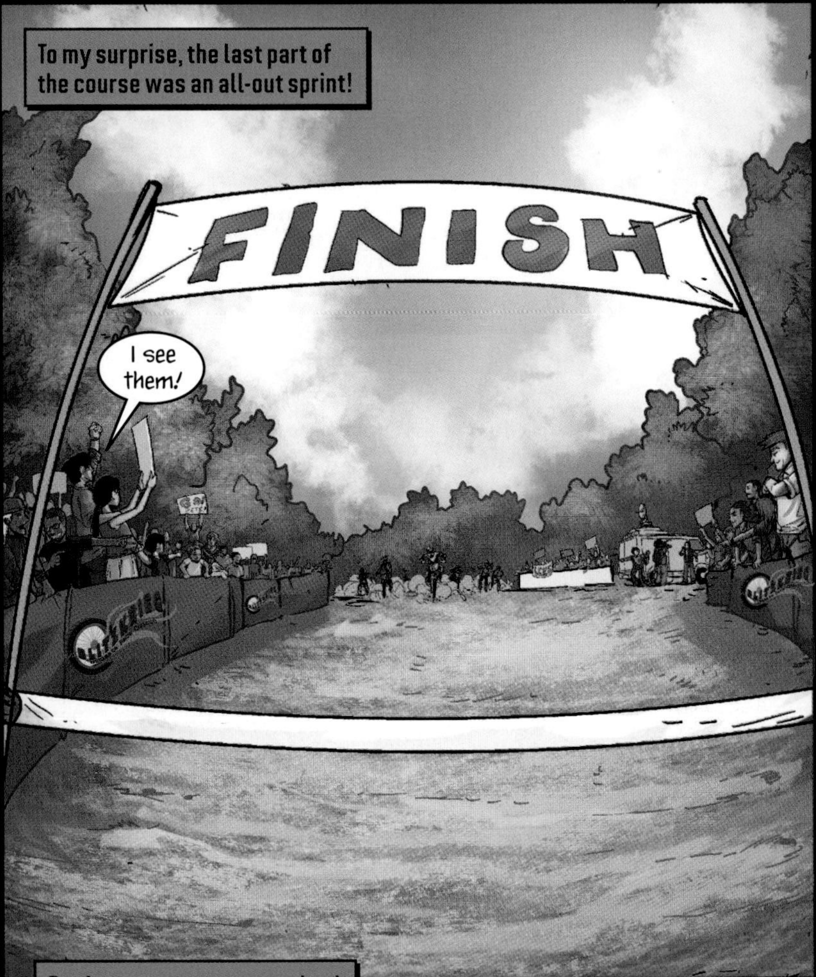
To my surprise, the last part of the course was an all-out sprint!
FINISH
I see them!

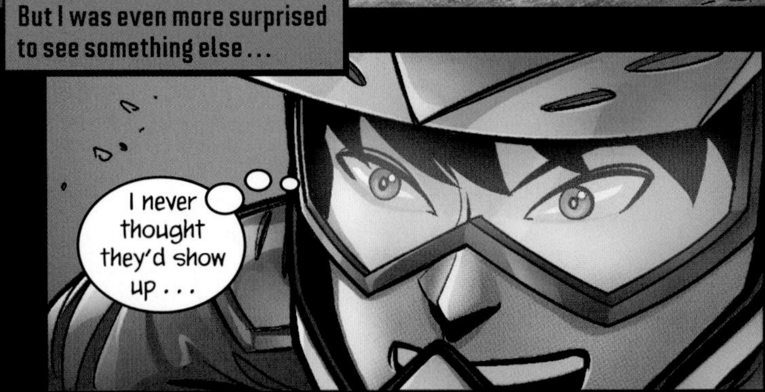
But I was even more surprised to see something else . . .
I never thought they'd show up . . .

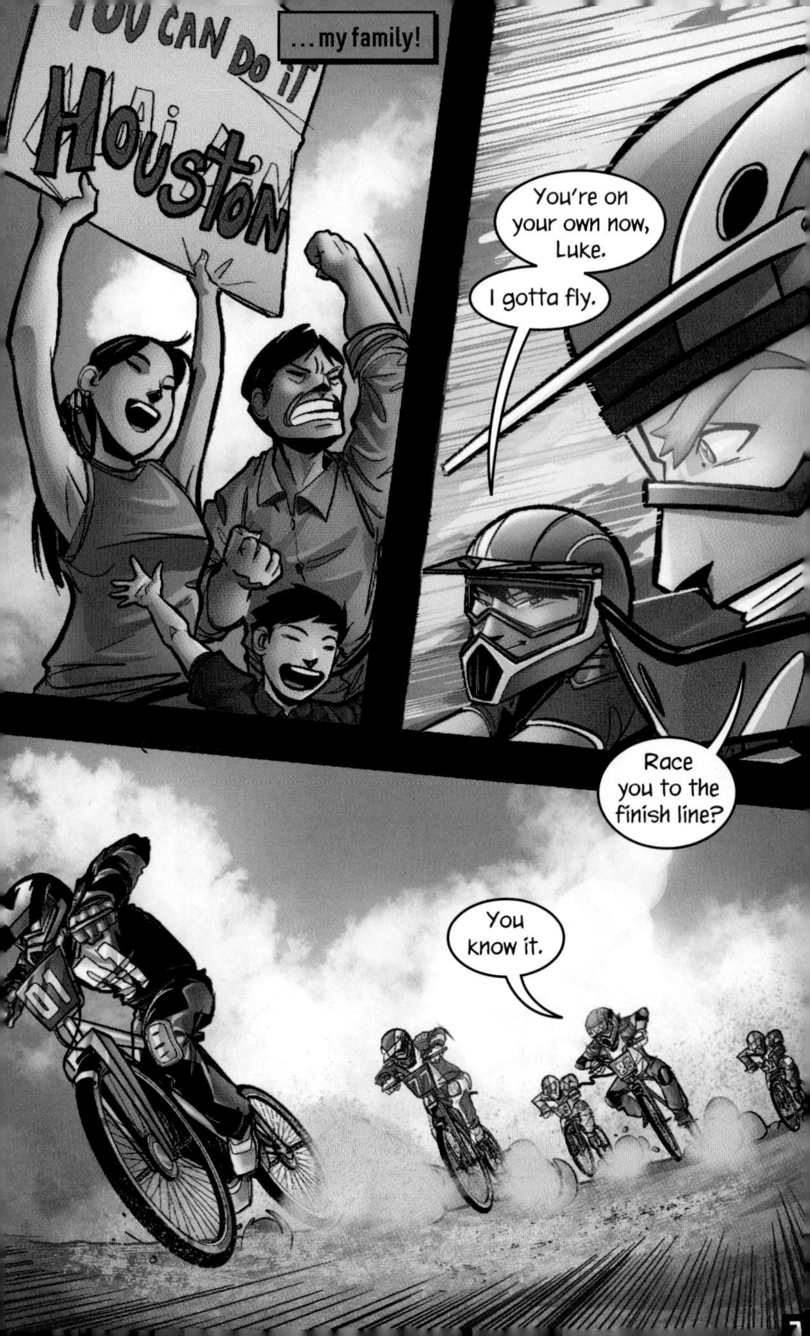
YOU CAN DO IT
Houston
... my family!
You're on your own now, Luke.
I gotta fly.
Race you to the finish line?
You know it.

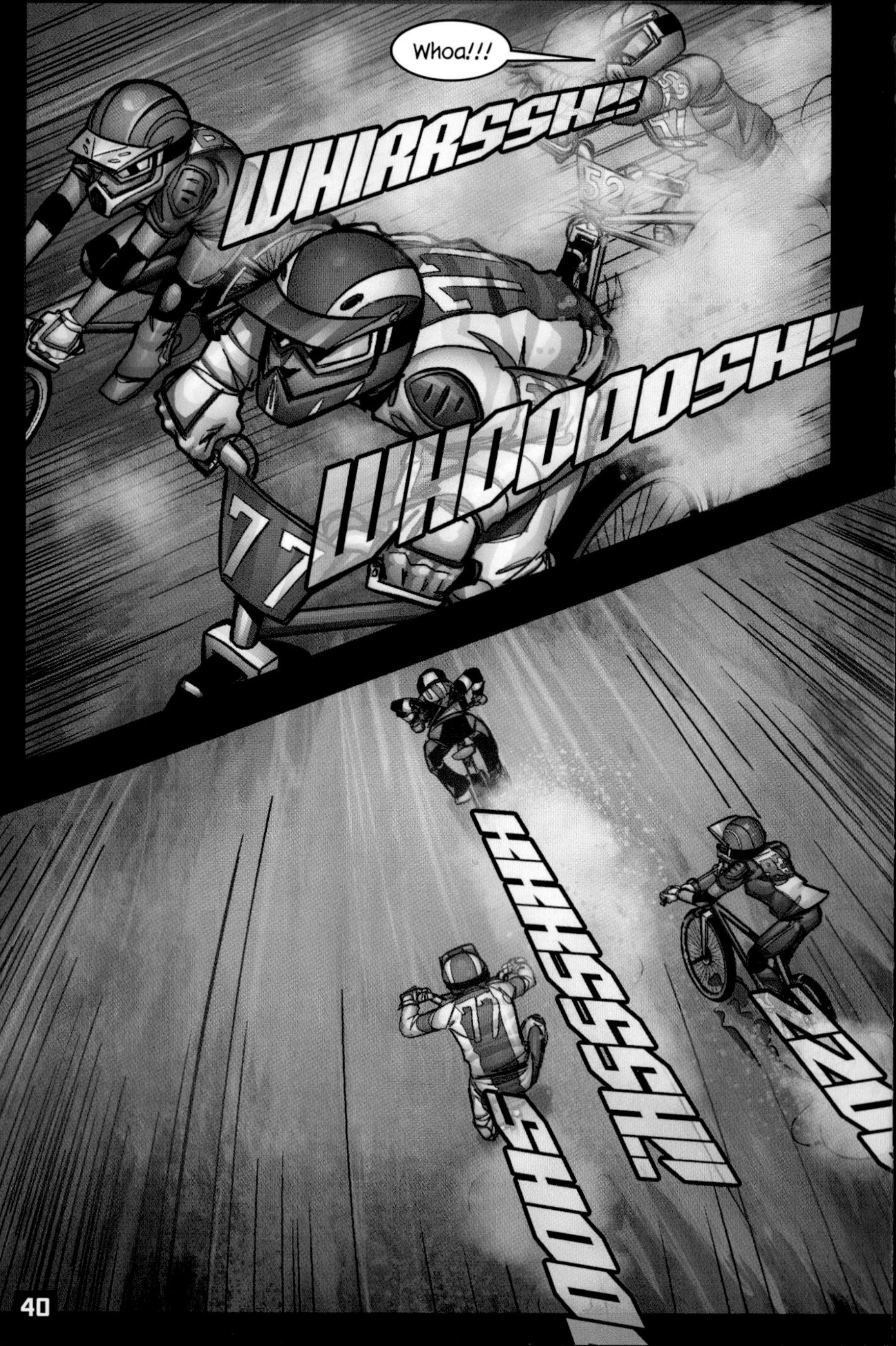
Whoa!!!
WHIRRSSH!!
WHOOOOSH!!

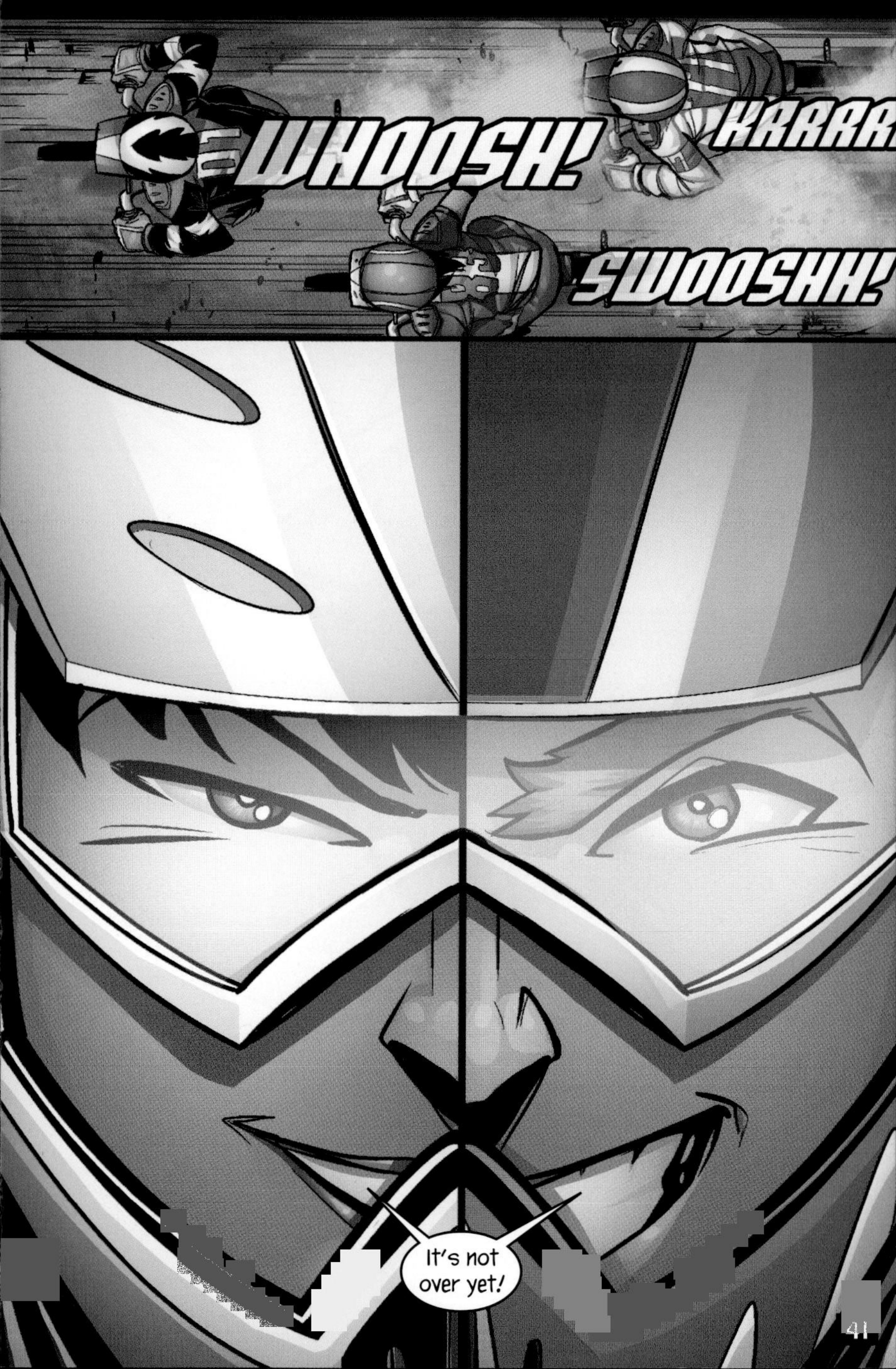
WHOOSH!
KRRRR
SWOOSHH!
It's not over yet!

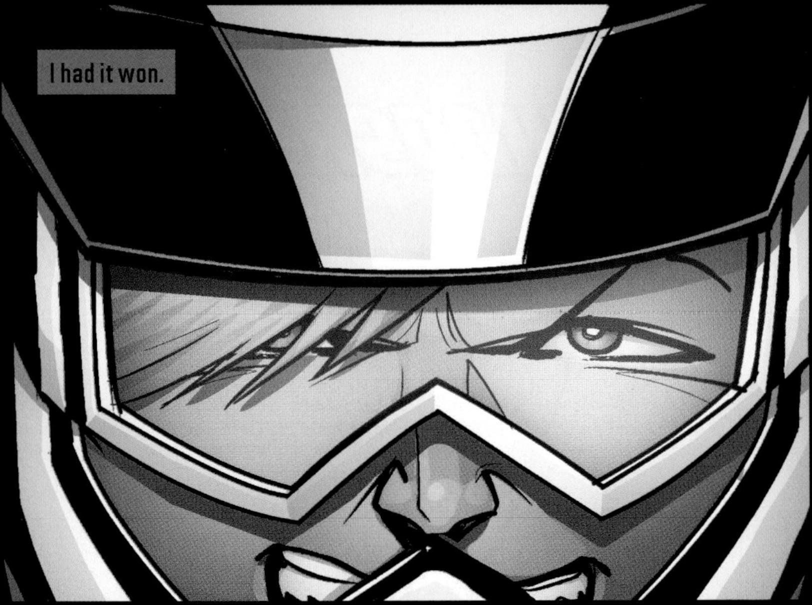
I had it won.

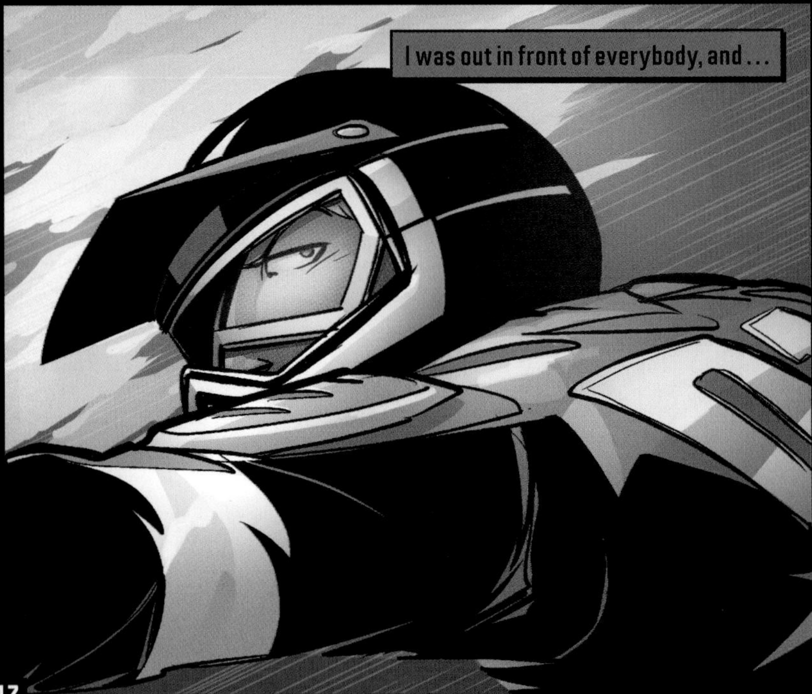
I was out in front of everybody, and . . .

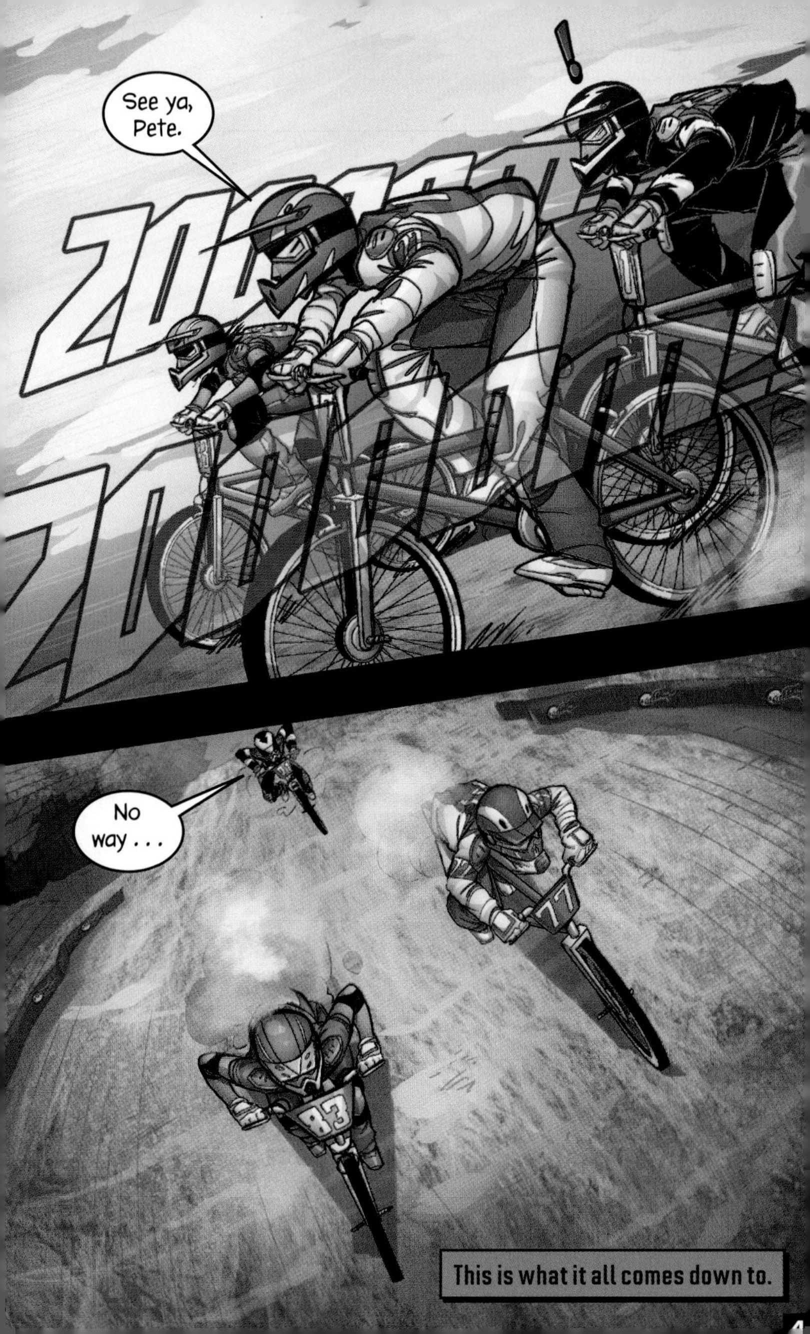
!
See ya, Pete.
No way . . .
This is what it all comes down to.

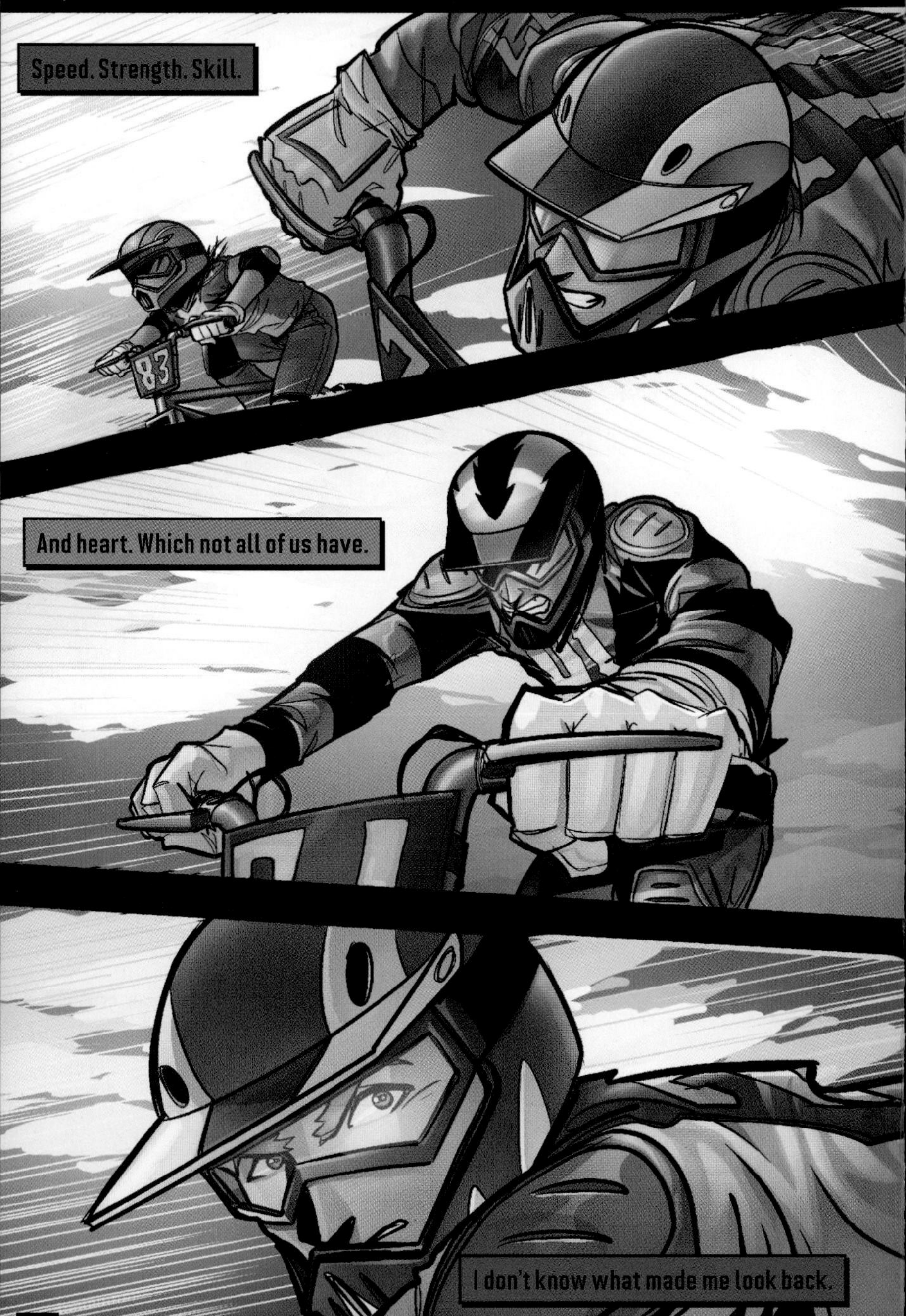
Speed. Strength. Skill.
83
And heart. Which not all of us have.
I don't know what made me look back.

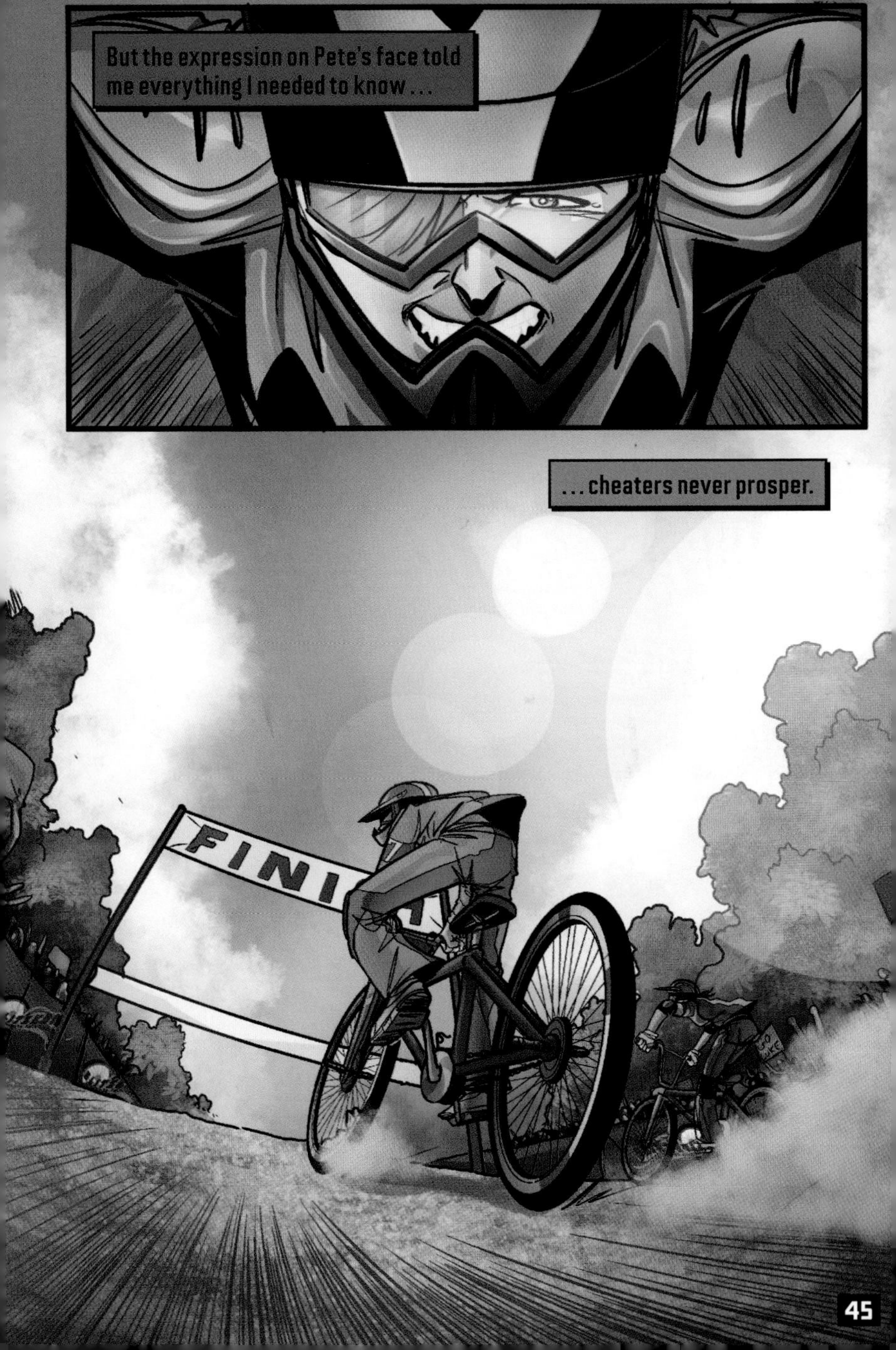
But the expression on Pete's face told me everything I needed to know . . .
. . . cheaters never prosper.
FINI

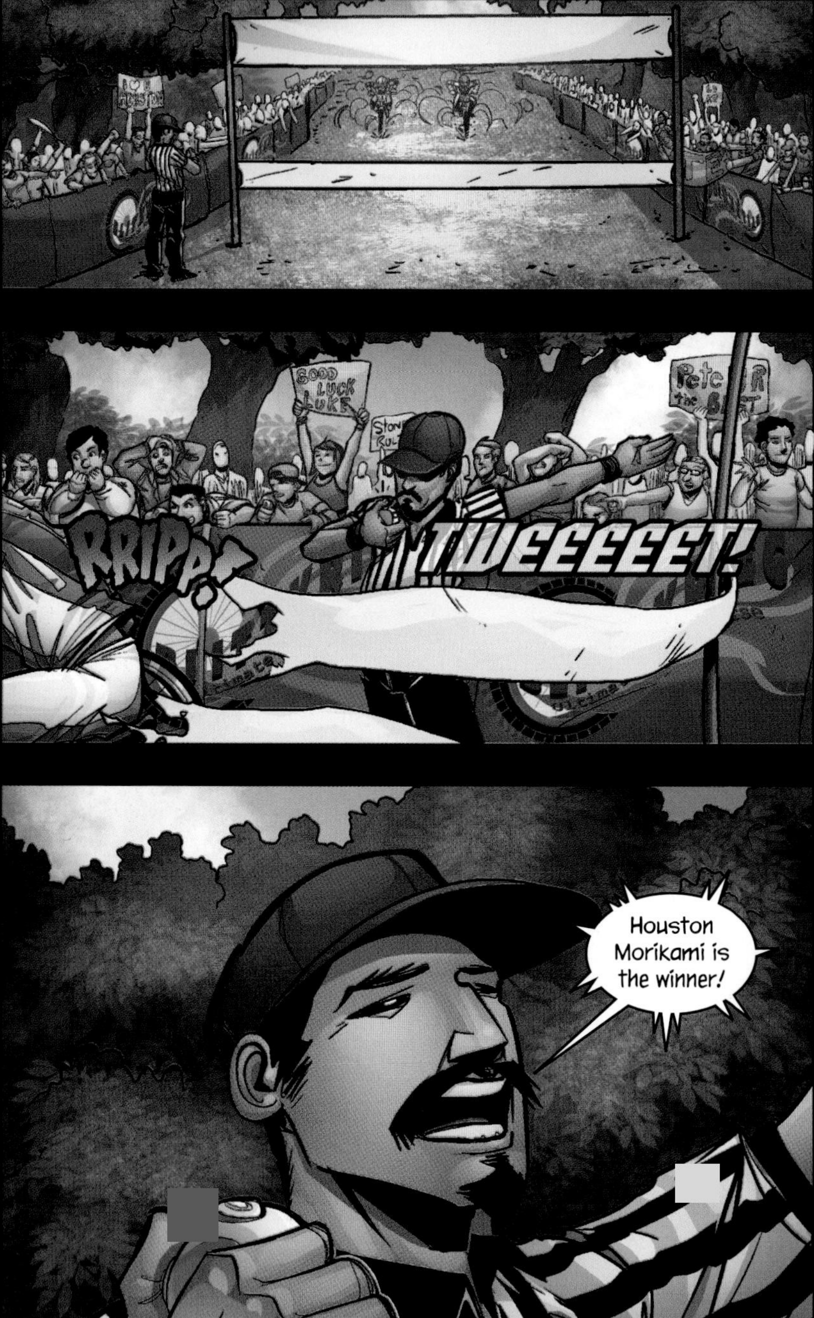
GOOD LUCK LUKE
RRIPP!
TWEEEEEET!
Houston Morikami is the winner!

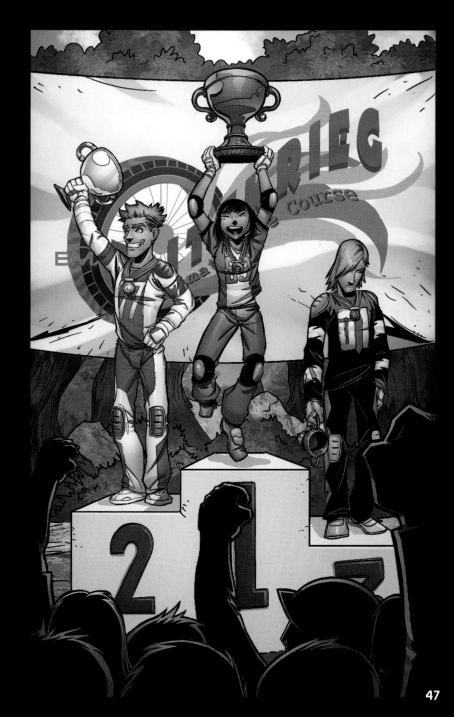

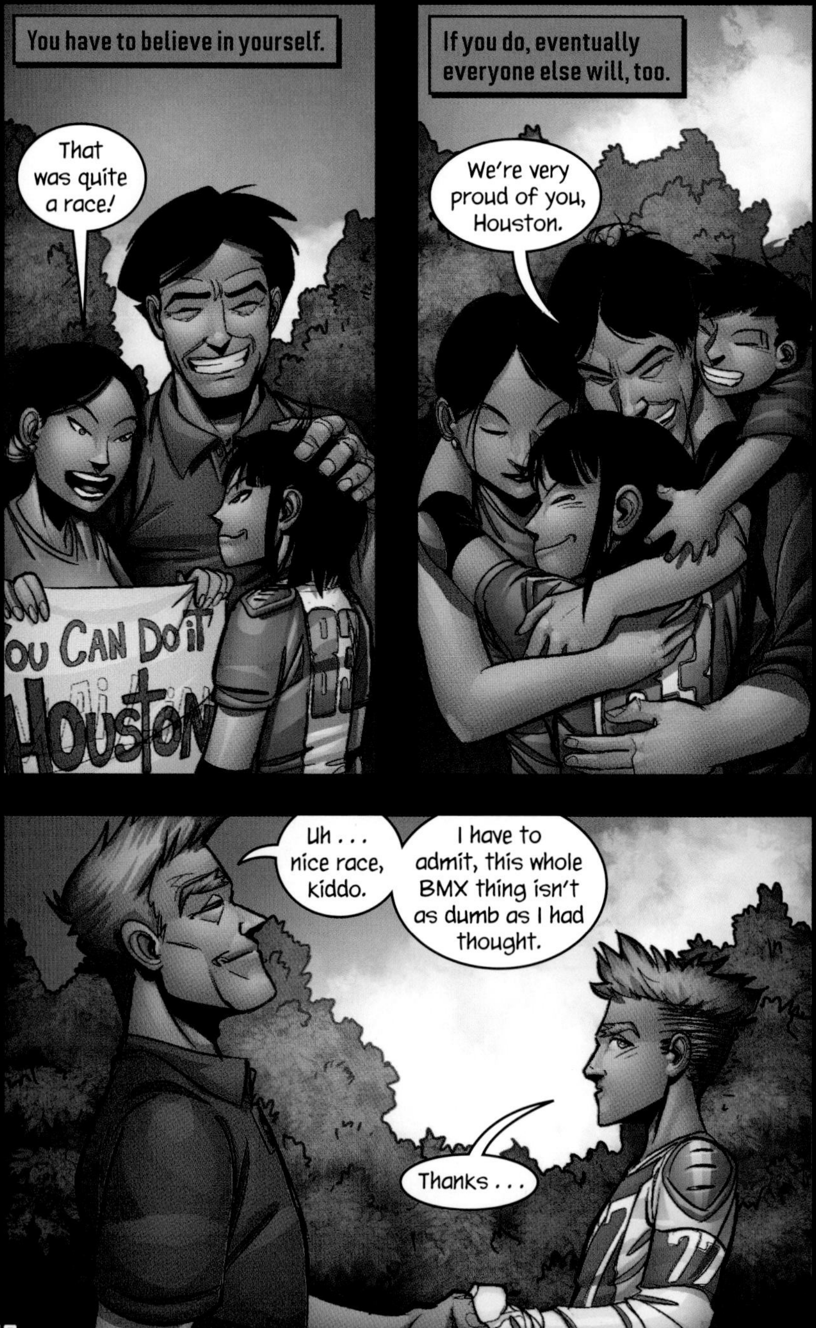
You have to believe in yourself.
That was quite a race!
YOU CAN DO it HOUSTON
If you do, eventually everyone else will, too.
We're very proud of you, Houston.
Uh . . . nice race, kiddo.
I have to admit, this whole BMX thing isn't as dumb as I had thought.
Thanks . . .

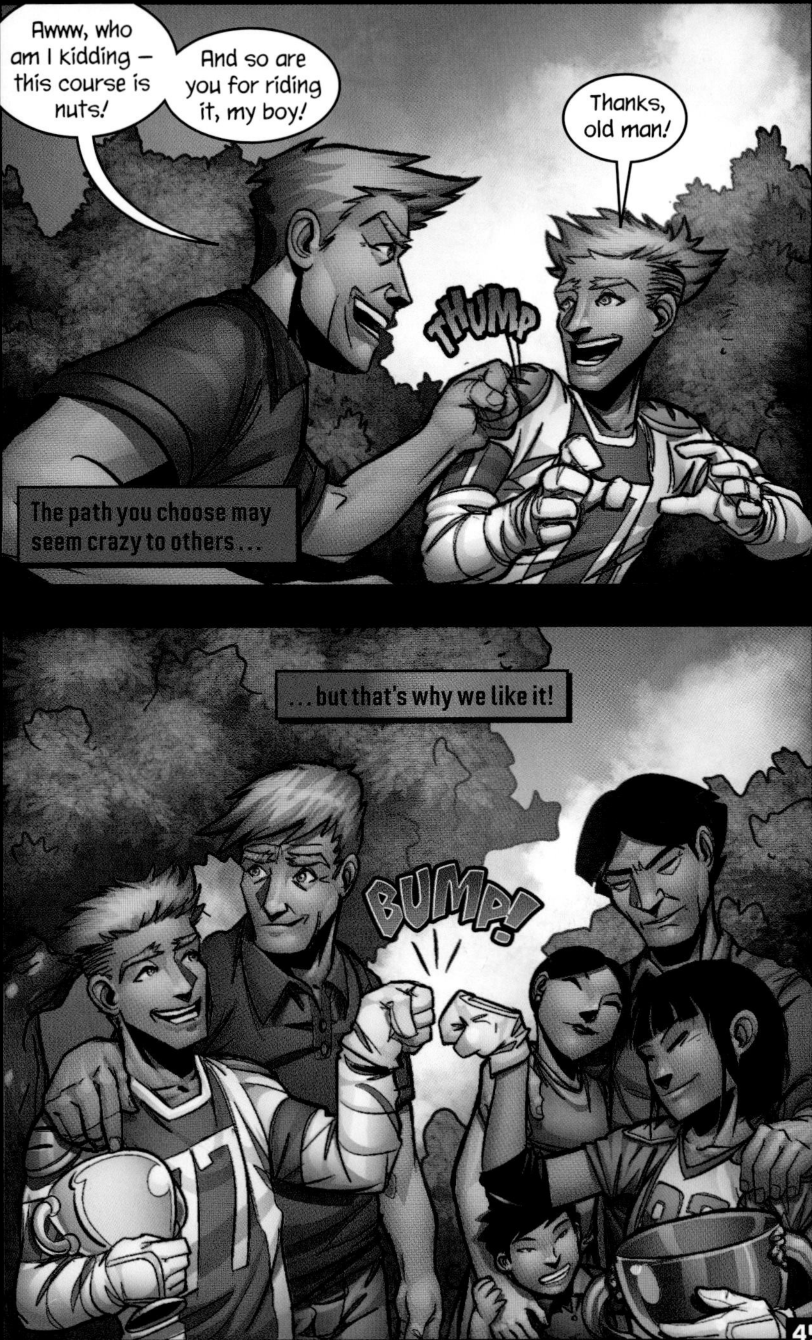
Awww, who am I kidding — this course is nuts!
And so are you for riding it, my boy!
Thanks, old man!
THUMP
The path you choose may seem crazy to others . . .
. . . but that's why we like it!
BUMP!

SPORTS ZONE
POSTGAME RECAP

BMX
BMX RACING

PNT
PAINTBALL

FBL
FOOTBALL

BSL
BASEBALL

BBL
BASKETBALL

HKY

HEATED RACE ENDS WITH SOLE GIRL CLAIMING GOLD!

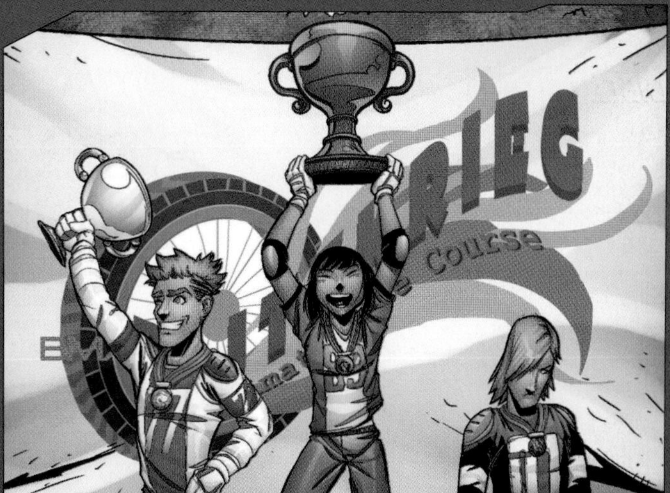

BY THE NUMBERS

FINAL STANDINGS:

FIRST: H. MORIKAMI
SECOND: L. LAWLESS
THIRD: P. HILDEBRAND

STORY: Houston Morikami managed to fend off Luke Lawless and lay claim to first place. The two racers were neck and neck until the final sprint. Houston was able to pull ahead and take the lead — and she never looked back. When asked about how it felt to beat the boys in the BMX-Blitzkrieg, Houstan said, "Whether you're a girl or a guy doesn't matter — I'm racing myself out there, anyway."

BLZ vs BKS 3-1
TGR vs RDR 33-32
EAG vs BAN 14-7
SPA vs WLD 4-3
BAN vs RDR 21-15
RZR vs LIG 4-3
BLZ vs BKS

SZ POSTGAME EXTRA

WHERE *YOU* ANALYZE THE GAME!

BMX racing fans got a real treat today when Luke Lawless and Houston Morikami faced off against Peter Hildebrand in the BMX-Blitzkrieg! Let's go into the stands and ask some fans for their opinions on the day's events . . .

DISCUSSION QUESTION 1

Peter stole blueprints for the BMX-Blitzkrieg race course, which gave him an unfair advantage. What kind of punishment should he receive?

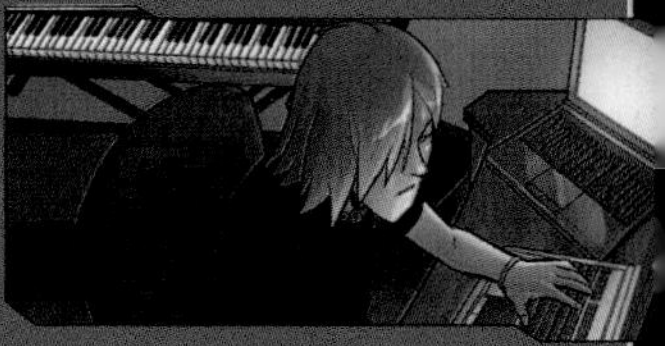

DISCUSSION QUESTION 2

Houston and Luke become friends while competing against each other. Do you think opponents should also be friends? Why or why not?

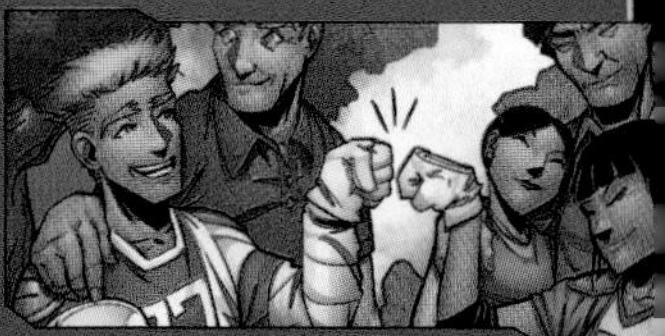

WRITING PROMPT 1

Luke and Houston's parents don't always understand them. In what ways do your parents "get" you? What kinds of things do they not understand? Write about it.

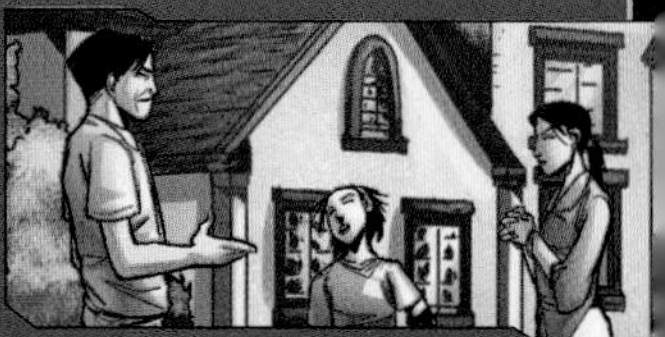

WRITING PROMPT 2

What is more important to you — winning or playing fair? Would you rather win and have no one cheer for you, or lose and have everyone on your side? Explain.

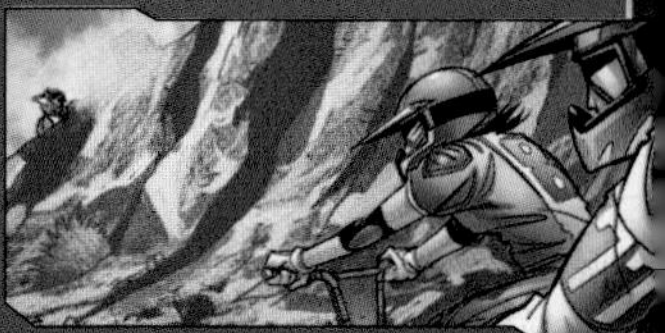

GLOSSARY

BLITZKRIEG (BLITZ-kreeg)—a German word meaning a swift attack

ENDORSEMENT (en-DORSS-ment)—if you have an endorsement, someone supports you and pays for your expenses in exchange for advertising

FLOCKED (FLOKD)—grouped up and traveled together

HESITATED (HEZ-uh-tate-id)—paused uncertainly before acting

INTENSE (in-TENSS)—very strong

PROSPER (PROSS-pur)—to be successful or thrive

QUALIFIED (KWAL-uh-fyed)—met the needs that allowed you to do something, like participate in a competition

RUTHLESS (ROOTH-liss)—cruel or without pity

ULTIMATE (UHL-tuh-mit)—last or final or best

CREATORS

SCOTT CIENCIN › Author

Scott Ciencin is a *New York Times* bestselling author of children's and adult fiction. He has written comic books, trading cards, video games, television shows, as well as many non-fiction projects. He lives in Sarasota, Florida with his beloved wife, Denise, and his best buddy, Bear, a golden retriever. He loves writing books for Stone Arch, and is working hard on many more that are still to come.

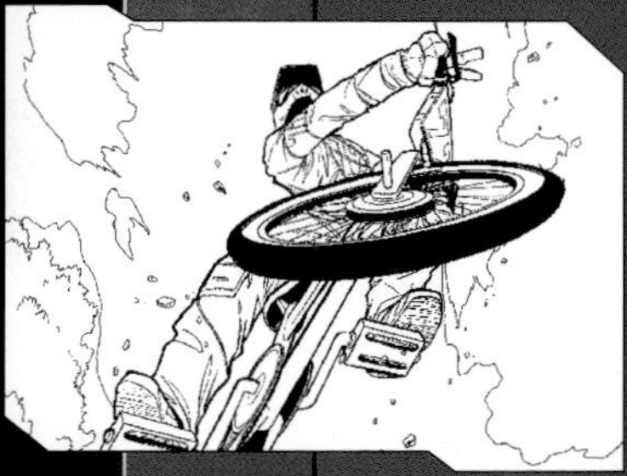

ABURTOV › Illustrator

Aburtov has worked in the comic book industry for more than 11 years. In that time, he has illustrated popular characters like Wolverine, Iron Man, Blade, and the Punisher. Recently, Aburtov started his own illustration studio called Graphikslava. He lives in Monterrey, Mexico, with his daughter, Ilka, and his beloved wife. Aburtov enjoys spending his spare time with family and friends.

ANDRES ESPARZA › Inker

Andres Esparza has been a graphic designer, colorist, and illustrator for many different companies and agencies. Andres now works as a full-time artist for Graphikslava studio in Monterrey, Mexico. In his spare time, Andres loves to play basketball, hang out with family and friends, and listen to good music.

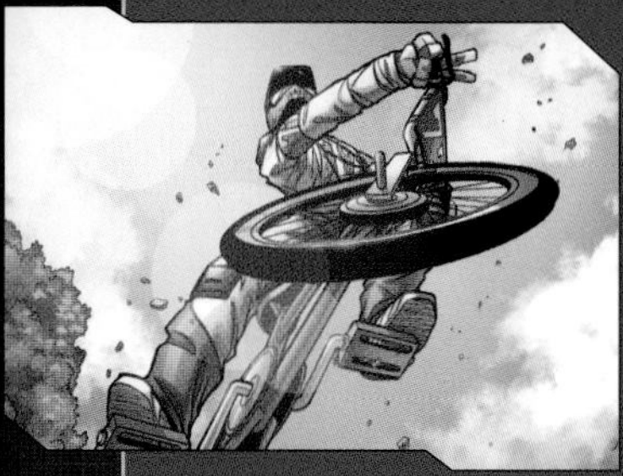

FARES MAESE › Colorist

Fares Maese is a graphic designer and illustrator. He has worked as a colorist for Marvel Comics, and as a concept artist for the card and role-playing games *Pathfinder* and *Warhammer*. Fares loves spending time playing video games with his Graphikslava comrades, and he's an awesome drum player.

Sports Illustrated KIDS
GRAPHIC NOVELS
QUICK COMIC

JAKE "SULLY" SULLIVAN IN:
TRACK TEAM TITANS

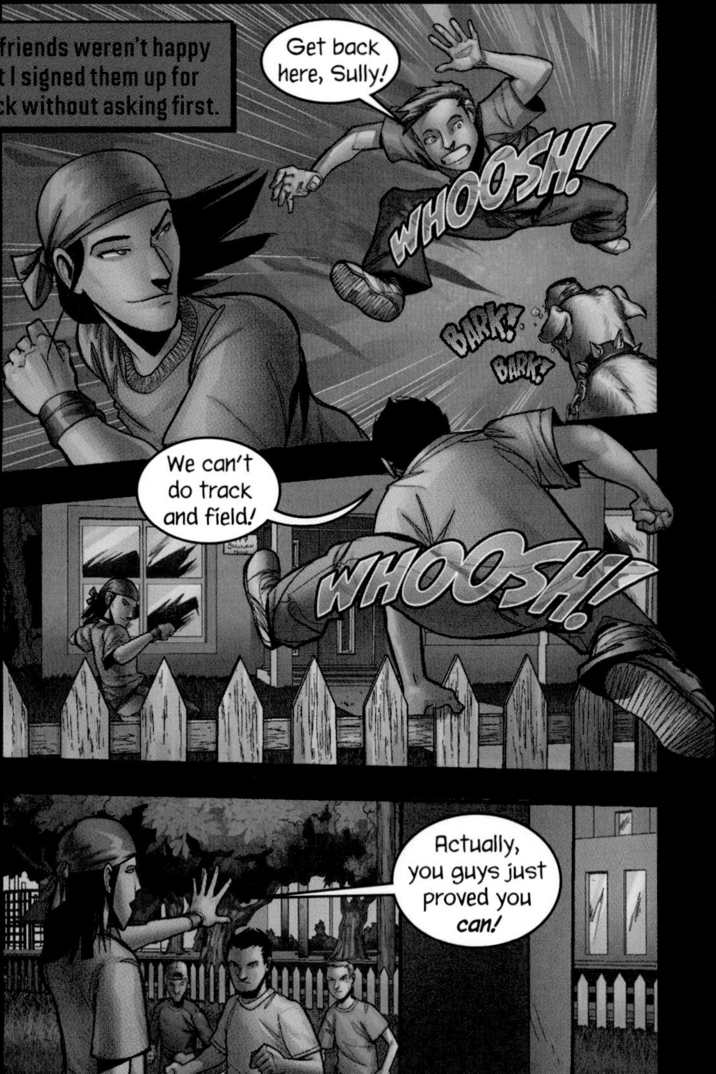
My friends weren't happy that I signed them up for track without asking first.
Get back here, Sully!
WHOOSH!
BARK!
BARK!
We can't do track and field!
WHOOSH!
Actually, you guys just proved you can!

» LOVE THIS QUICK COMIC? READ THE WHOLE STORY IN TRACK TEAM TITANS – ONLY FROM STONE ARCH BOOKS!

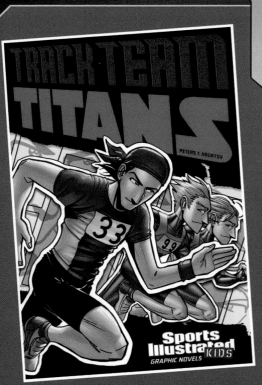
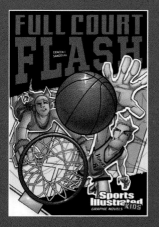

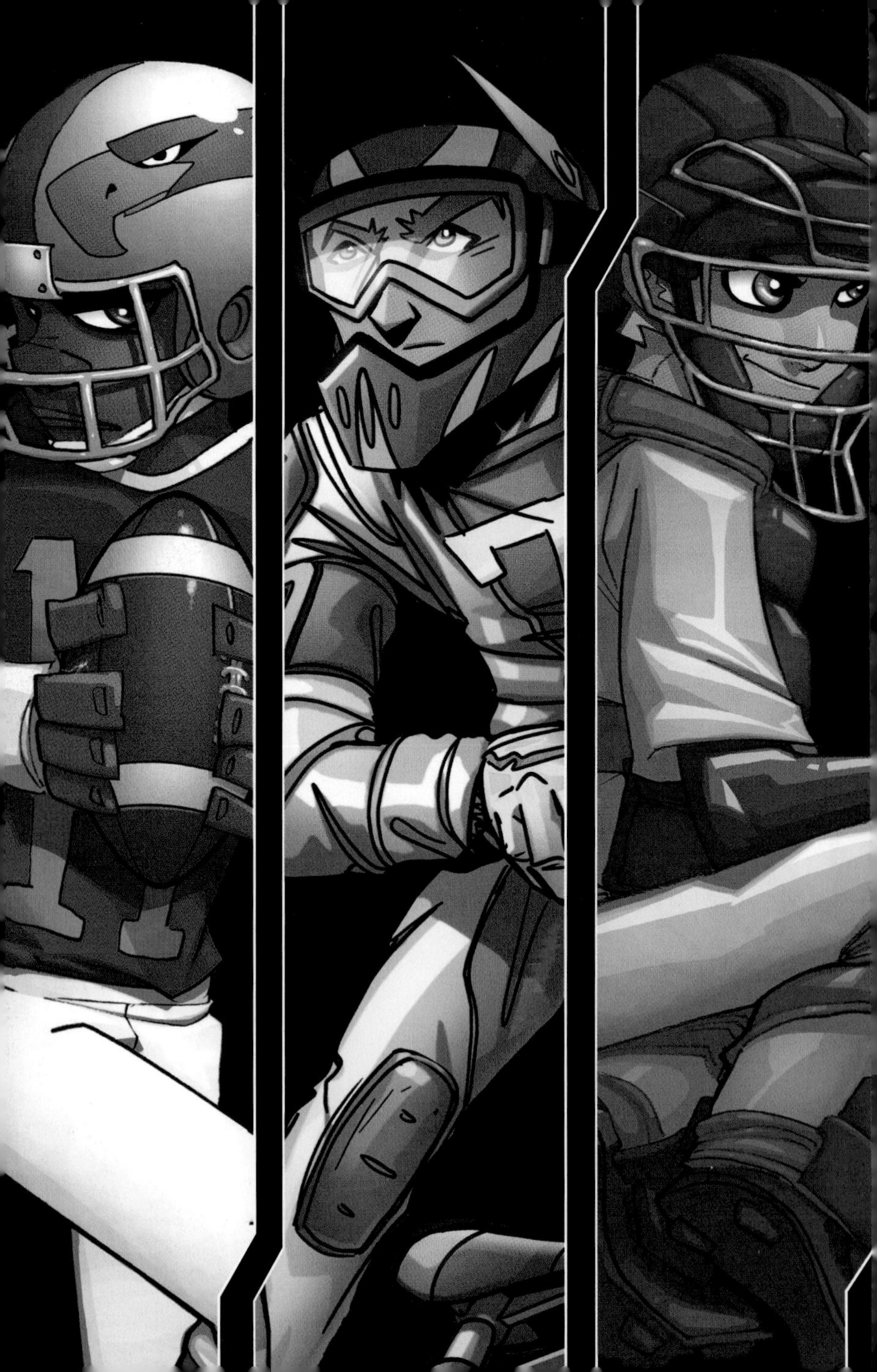